DAMAGE & OTHER STORIES

POORNIMA MANCO

For my father, who taught me the value of patience.

"The two most powerful warriors are patience and time" - Leo Tolstoy.

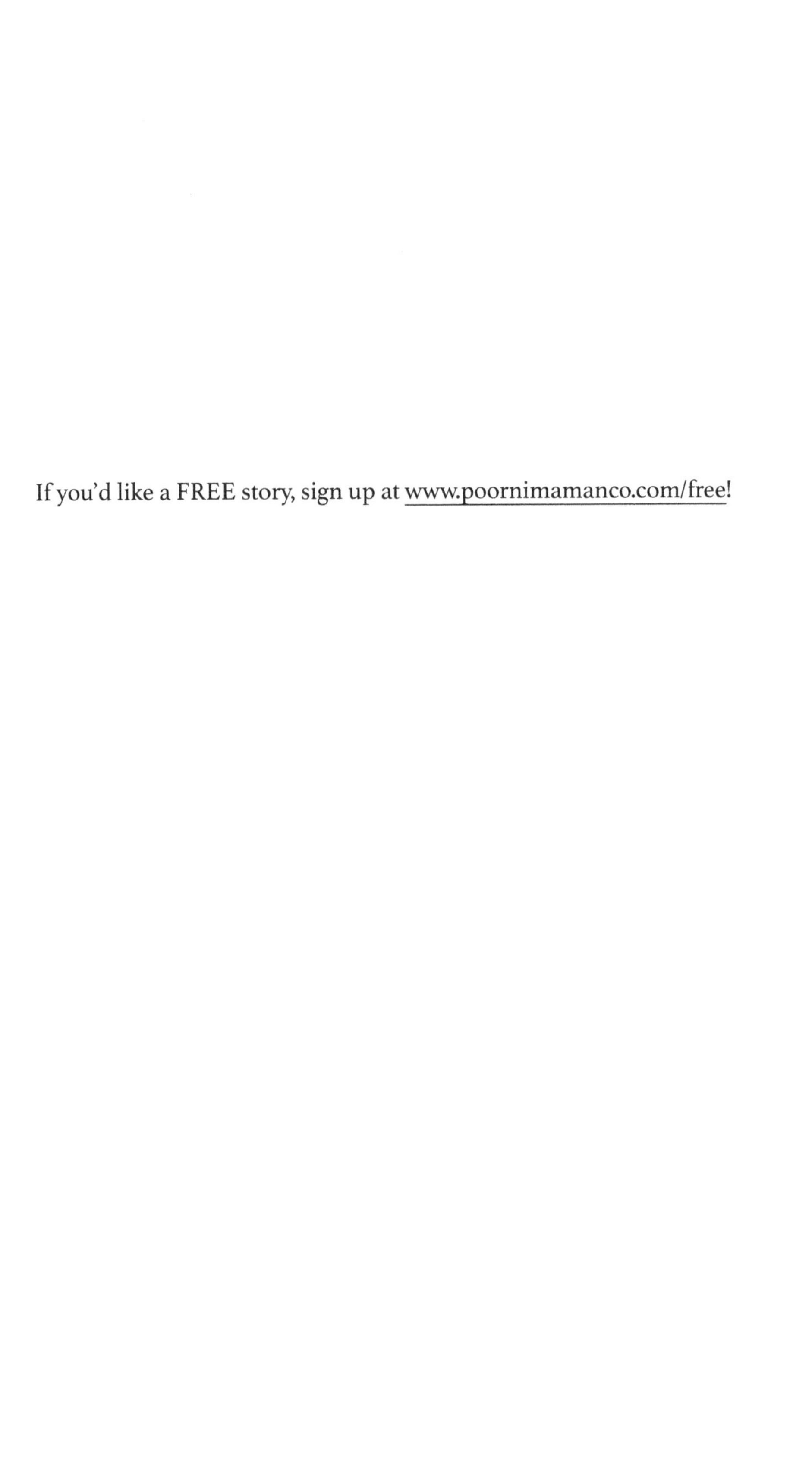

If you'd like a FREE story, sign up at <u>www.poornimamanco.com/free</u>!

CONTENTS

1
____

DAMAGE

A T fifty two I fell in love again. It started out as a challenge, a pitting of wits and ended with us being devastatingly, terribly, foolishly in love. Of course, neither of us had planned for it to happen, and that is what made it so surprising. Isn't fifty two when you get ready to hang up your boots and smoke that pipe? And here I was, lusting after a woman who was married. Perhaps her very unavailability made her so attractive, or the fact that I, for once, had come across someone who filled that void in me.

Anyhow, this story is not about a lost love, it is about a lost child. And lost opportunities.

"KALYAN, THIS IS SODA." Our hostess introduced me to the languid eyed woman at a ridiculous Delhi 'do' I had been compelled to attend.

"Soda? What kind of a name is that?" I sneered at her, immediately taking in the cupid's bow lips, the backless *choli*,[1] held together by a single knot, the waist length hair that swung in a plait.

"It's short for Saudamini." She responded huskily, refusing to rise to the bait. "I read your column. It's very interesting. I asked Mita for an introduction. I am a writer too. Oh, nothing major...just a few poems..."

I cringed inwardly, as this was definitely a prelude to getting me to read her stuff.

"No, no." She laughed, sensing my discomfiture. "I have no intention of displaying my rather amateurish writing to you. But I did want to question you about a point you made the other day..."

AND SO IT STARTED. A friendship, I would tell myself, denying my physical response to her. I refused to touch her. Never once did I let my hand graze hers. Never did I lean in close enough to smell her perfume. Not at the beginning anyhow. Then there was the husband. A nice fellow. The devoted sort. I had a grudging admiration for him. To have found and held a woman like that required gumption.

She had a child. A son with learning disabilities. She was slightly embarrassed by him. As though it was her fault. As though her womb had refused to cooperate, and produced a faulty product, and therefore she must be to blame, for it was *her* womb. I was embarrassed for her. I saw it as regressive and pointless. Yet, our friendship grew.

Over coffees and sneaked cigarettes, we discussed politics and books. Over dinners that turned cold, we had heated arguments over religion. She believed in god, karma, prayer. I didn't. Rajesh, the husband, took note of the sparks, but he was used to indulging her. He was also used to her sudden obsessions and their quick souring.

"How can an educated, obviously intelligent woman like you believe that some entity whose existence hasn't been proven, controls our destiny?"

"Because I have faith. Incidents in my life have steered me to believe."

"What sorts of incidents? Examples?"

She refused to be drawn, turning away in a huff towards the kitchen. I watched her go, exasperated and aroused in equal measure. After each of our arguments, I wished to make love to her. To grind into her and watch her face contort in ecstasy. Instead I made do with another cigarette.

Rajesh joined me outside. He didn't smoke, but brought out his beer. We sat in companionable silence, enjoying the balmy evening. The sunset had unleashed a myriad of hues in the sky, and the bougainvillea bush seemed to be on fire, the crimson bouncing off the magenta flowers, seeking to envelop each one of the surrounding plants in its reflected glory.

"I worry about Akash, K."

"Why? He seems to be doing fine. Have there been any problems lately?"

"Well, the school called. He's been getting into fights with the other boys. He attacked one with a pair of scissors the other day."

"What?! That's so unlike Akash. He seems such a gentle boy..."

"He was provoked. The other child had been calling him names, picking on him. I guess he just lost the plot."

"That can happen with anyone. I mean, surely the school recognises that? Of course, he needs disciplining but Akash, of all kids, needs to be handled with care. Have you spoken to anyone in authority?"

"Yes, we have. We're trying to organise a counsellor. But there's more...he's been soiling himself, and the bed wetting has started again. For a fourteen-year-old, that's not good news."

I agreed. I also wondered at this sudden unburdening. I was used to Rajesh being in the background. Soda was always the focal point of these meetings. Yet, she studiously avoided all mention of Akash's issues. As though glossing over the obvious would somehow make it go away.

Akash himself was an interesting study. He was taller than his mother. Overweight and extremely acne prone. A slightly foul smell followed him around, and he had no friends to speak of. Our very brief interactions consisted of me greeting him with an overly hearty "Hello my boy, how goes it?" and him responding with a grunt. Now and again, when our eyes accidentally met, I would get a glimpse of a very small, frightened child, unable to cope with the horrors of the world around him.

"HOW IS THE COUNSELLING GOING?" I asked Soda, a few weeks later over our rum and cokes.

"What counselling?" She spluttered, wide eyed.

"Akash's of course. Rajesh had mentioned..."

She turned apoplectic.

"There is NOTHING wrong with Akash!! Boys will be boys. I wish people would stop judging us!"

I knew then to leave well enough alone.

AS THE DELHI Summer turned into a golden Autumn, I found my visits to their house increasing in frequency. I had only an empty apartment with an old, deaf ayah for company. The food she cooked was unpalatable, and her cleaning was cursory at best. Where my books had been my constant companions, I searched for a human connection now. Soda, with all her faults, was an alluring woman. She could sense I was drawn to her, and felt flattered. Yet, I was only the nth man responding to her beauty and her warmth.

"K, why have you never married?"

"Are you going to set me up Soda? Please don't! I find these things excruciating..."

"Don't answer my question with a question!"

"Well," I leaned back on the sofa, and looked at Akash who sat in front of the Television, utterly engrossed, his hand moving into the packet of crisps, and back to his mouth with robotic regularity. "I just never met the right person."

She looked at me from under her lashes, a coy look that she had perfected. "What kind of person?"

I knew she wanted me to say someone like her.

"Someone who agrees with me about religion being a pile of nonsense."

Rajesh guffawed from the kitchen. He returned with his drink, and we raised our glasses to each other in a surreptitious complicity.

"Sunil is coming next week." Soda intercepted our silent communication. "He'll stay a few days with us."

I had heard about her brother and his hell raising ways. A politician's lackey, he was accustomed to throwing his weight about and very few people crossed him.

"Sunil *Mamu*[2] is coming?" Akash asked excitedly. It was the first time I had seen him excited about anything other than his computer games. "Do you think he'll let me play with his guns again?"

Soda smiled at him indulgently. "I think he might let you touch them. But really Akash, you are too young to play with them."

"Guns? Am I hearing this right?" I looked at Rajesh, appalled.

"Oh, he has a license and everything. Besides, it's a bit of a hobby with him. He's part of Lokesh Sharma's entourage, and you know how it is, with these politicians and their followers."

I felt a sudden unease to be in the midst of people who treated weapons that could maim and slaughter, so casually. I was a man of letters. Words were my weaponry and my armour.

"... but you must come K! I'll do a nice dinner. Sunil is great company."

I doubted that we would have much in common. I nearly concocted a prior appointment. Yet, one look at Soda's expectant face, made all my arguments melt away. What was it about this woman that I could not resist?

IT WAS the Sunday that changed everything. The party was already in full swing when I arrived. Rajesh was playing bartender, and Soda the consummate hostess. But all eyes were on the tall, beefy man who sat holding court in their living room. Sunil gave off an air of importance. A 'don't mess with me or you'll disappear' aura. I guess, in the power hungry circles of Delhi, that was an undeniable part of his attraction.

I nursed my single malt, as I tried to stay inconspicuous. I simply could not get into it with this man. Our ideologies were so far removed from one another, it was as though we belonged to two different planets. So, I let him wax eloquent on the subject of politics and power play, as he saw it. Mentally, I bracketed him a fool and an ignoramus.

"What do you think K?" asked Rajesh pointedly of another badass, throwaway comment of his brother-in-law's.

"I don't." I replied obliquely.

"Are you too high and mighty to get involved in the discussion Mr Bhushan?" A mightily sozzled Sunil raised himself up and staggered towards me. "The mountain is coming to Mohammad... Tell me, doesn't that column of yours talk about the sectarian violence the last political party instigated?"

"Yes." I answered calmly.

"Then don't you agree with what our party wants? Parity for all? Justice for all?"

"I agree with the principles, yes."

"Good man! I knew we would see eye to eye. Get him another drink!" He enveloped me in a bear hug, reeking of alcohol, staleness and some expensive aftershave. "I need to go pee."

I silently congratulated myself for ducking that one. I went outside for a smoke. Soda followed shortly after.

"You don't like him."

I smiled and inhaled the smoke deeply.

"I don't like most people. Don't take it personally."

"Hmmm," she paused for a moment, looking at me intently, "I've written something I'd like you to see. If you don't mind."

"Soda, I don't do poetry. I've told you before. I couldn't critique it if my life depended on it."

"But it doesn't! All I'm asking for is a bit of feedback."

"Couldn't you just post it on Facebook or something? Isn't there an audience for that sort of thing?"

"K, why must you always be so unyielding?"

I opened my mouth to answer, but a shriek from the living room cut me short.

The AK-47 lay on the coffee table, as incongruous as a swan in a battlefield.

People milled around it, as though a celebrity had just been spotted. Some leaned forward to touch it reverently. Others admired it from a distance. The smug owner did little to disguise his delight.

"That's my Kalashnikov...my pride and joy." Sunil stood back, swaying slightly.

"Can I touch it *Mamu*[3]?" Akash asked nervously.

"Of cour..."

"NO!" I cut in and grabbed Akash by his arm, and dragged him towards his room.

"K! What are you doing?" cried Soda.

Sunil looked at me and started laughing. "Scared of guns, big guy?"

I ignored him and looked over at Rajesh. He swirled the ice in his glass, refusing to meet my eyes.

Akash struggled against my grip. I refused to relent. His gaze was vicious as I sat him on his bed and tried to explain fruitlessly.

"Akash...guns...they are bad things...they injure...they kill...You are so young...this is not for you to see..."

"Akash, go to bed!" Soda's voice was like a whiplash. "K, I think it's time for you to leave."

The party was dispersing as I made my way out. I was nearly at my car, when she caught up with me.

"I know you think I'm an irresponsible mother, a callous one even. But you don't understand. Anything that brings a bit of joy into my son's life, I cannot, I will not deny him that."

Her lips quivered as she looked up at me, and in that mad moment, I leaned forward and kissed her hard. She resisted at first, and then, with a desperate hunger kissed me back. Her tongue probing, seeking, finding. She pulled away just as suddenly. Her eyes were as wide as saucers. She turned and ran back home, leaving me hungry and dissatisfied.

Hungry and dissatisfied. That was my lot.

·　·　·

I DIDN'T HEAR from them for the next few weeks. I guessed then that the tenuous friendship had come to its natural end. A part of me was relieved. Another part missed her fiercely. I buried myself in work. Looming deadlines and long forgotten books once again became my *raison d'être*. I reasoned this was the best way. The only way.

Her appearance at my door was a shock. She wore a pale pink shirt and a floaty skirt of some kind.

"Is Asha here?"

Asha, my maid, was having her afternoon siesta. I nodded dumbly.

She took my hand and led me into the bedroom.

There was never any doubt in my mind that I did what I did out of love. My worship of her body was just an extension of that love. As we lay together; entwined, spent; I refused to ask why. Her being there was enough.

ASHA'S siestas and our rendezvous became synonymous. While my maid slept, I awoke to pleasure and to pain. There was a time, when just holding her would have been a dream come true. How soon I forgot that. I wanted so much more now. I wanted her - all of her. These snatched moments whetted my appetite for a life together.

"Leave him."

"I can't," she sighed, "I have no reason to. He's a good husband, and a good father. I love him too, K. Can't we just be content with this?"

No! I wanted to shout. But I lay there, quietly, letting her nestle into me. Her hair tickling my chest. Her foot running up and down my leg absently.

"Has Rajesh asked where you go every afternoon?"

"He thinks I'm at a book club with some friends. Besides, work is busy. He is too preoccupied to care. But he does ask about you. He misses you K. You're one of the few men whose company he likes."

I laughed at the irony.

"What a cosy threesome we are!"

"Come over. In fact, come tonight! Why don't you? It could be like the old times..."

I looked at her wonderingly.

"Soda, are you naive or are you deliberately ignoring the fact that it will never be like the old times? I wasn't fucking you in the old times!"

"Oh stop it K! You don't have to be so crude."

I let myself get persuaded to go. More because I couldn't bear to be apart from her. If that meant swallowing my pride, and watching her play *hausfrau*, I was willing to do that too.

I WAS astounded at the change in Akash. He seemed bigger in size, but somehow diminished. He skulked around the house, throwing me venomous looks.

"There have been more problems, K," Rajesh confided, "Group of class bullies have been picking on him incessantly. Trouble is, one of them is Lokesh Sharma's son. The school is treading very carefully."

"Why not just move him? There must be other schools?"

"Mid-term? With his Board exams coming up? Where K? We are stuck between a rock and a hard place."

"Can't Sunil do something? I mean, he's in the inner circle, isn't he? Surely he could have a word with the father?"

Rajesh looked at me quizzically. "These people don't talk K. You should know that. This is some jumped up hoodlum with too much power, and too little sense. Sunil has already washed his hands of the matter."

Dinner was a tense affair. The old familiarity had disappeared for a variety of reasons. Yet, every time I looked over at Soda, desire coursed through my veins. I could scarcely disguise it and excused myself as quickly as I could.

Akash came to the door to see me off.

"Uncle, I want to say something to you."

"Yes son?"

"Please don't call me son. I am not your son. And leave my mother alone."

I stood there, aghast. He lumbered off, leaving a toxic whiff in his wake.

"AKASH KNOWS." I let her in quietly.

"What?! How? When...?"

"I don't know. But he's warned me off."

"Don't be silly K. How could he know? He's at school, and I cover my tracks...Unless..."

"Unless what?"

"He was leafing through my diary the other day. Some poems I'd written...There's one about you...," She sat on the bed, her face pale. "He must have put two and two together. Oh K! What are we going to do?"

I took her hand in mine.

"Perhaps it's time to come clean? Maybe it's happened for a reason?"

"How can you say that?" she said, alarmed, "You want me to wreck the entire fabric of my life? Over an affair?"

"Is that all this is Soda? An affair?"

She was mute. The tears fell of their own accord.

"No," she whispered, "But I can't... It's too much to ask..."

I held her in my arms as she wept. I kissed her hair, impotent in my frustration.

She left soon after.

When I saw her next, she looked through me. She never looked *at* me again.

He creeps into the room. It is early morning, and the household is asleep. His uncle lies on the bed, arms akimbo, snoring loudly, the alcohol still working its soporific alchemy. The gun has been carelessly shoved under the bed. He slides it out silently, stroking the smooth metal as he does. He feels a rush; a quickening.

He wraps it quietly in layers of towels, and hides it in his rucksack, cleverly camouflaged by books and assorted sundries. He takes his father's photograph from the frame, and inserts it in his History book. He takes her diary and puts it alongside.

He showers then shovels his breakfast in. All the while, hiding his strange and delicious secret. No one sits with him on the school bus. He barely notices. It is how it's always been. But not for long.

Assembly is dull and monotonous. They shuffle in. Listen to the teachers, sing the anthem, shuffle out. There is a spring in his step. He waits for his moment. It will be perfect.

Classes rush by. Maths merges into Biology into English. Finally, there is a break. He carries his rucksack out, along with his tiffin. He sits in his usual spot under the tree and waits.

"Hey Fatso! What's sexy Mummy made for you today, huh?"

"Look, look...egg paratha[4]*... Mmmmm...tasty...wanna bite? Hey? What did you say? You're on a diet! Bloody right you are, Lardy bottom."*

"Rohit, look, snotty face is pulling out a towel to cry into...Ha ha!"

When they see the gun, their mouths fall open. At last, at long last, they see him. Him and the gun. The Gun and him.

He fires in rapid succession. Bullets spray them chop-chop, chop-chop, and their blood and gore and screams rent the air. The recoil is powerful, and he loses his balance, but doesn't let go of the gun. It keeps firing into the air, automatically discharging its barrel magazine like he is discharging his rage. At some point, he stops and looks at the carnage around him with a savage satisfaction.

There are people running towards him. Teachers, security staff, other students. He sees them coming and smiles. Then he turns the gun upon himself.

IT was the first of its kind in India. Our very own Columbine. And somewhere within me a cascade of guilt began its journey. I would recall that haunted little boy, and feel my stomach turn upon itself.

Why didn't I do more? Why didn't I listen? Why didn't I care? My love withered and died the same day as those children. It was replaced by a self-loathing so strong that nothing would ever take away its bilious taste. So many lives lay decimated. So many souls scarred. Those that died on that horrific day were the first casualties. Those that survived were the collateral damage. This was the price of hate. This was the price of love. This was the price of ignorance and arrogance. We would pay for it the rest of our lives.

2

SAMSARA

The heater shut out the exact moment her phone began to ring. For a moment she lay there, in the dark, heart thudding, listening to its shrill tone cut through the remainder of her night. Then she reached for it.

"Hello?"

"*Sahib*[1]*...sahib*...it's me, Narinder."

With an inward groan she sat up in bed, pulling her sliding duvet up to her chin.

"What is it?"

"We have been called to the Big Bangla. Something has happened."

This chased away the last of her sleep.

The Big Bangla belonged to the Forestry Minister. In actual fact, it was called Rhododendron House, but as most Indian tongues couldn't get to grips with it, it was reduced to being called the Big House or the Big Bangla.

"Is it okay if I bring the jeep around?"

"Yes," she sighed impatiently, "Give me ten minutes."

Narinder was wrapped up warm, and the monkey cap he wore only revealed his startling green eyes, crusted as they were with sleep and the remnants of cheap whiskey. The eyes did their usual run over her person, lingering on her nonexistent bosom that she vainly tried to hide under layers of wool. Impatiently she gestured for him to drive.

"So, what's happened?"

"Don't know Sahib. There was a call to the *Thana*[2]. Police Constable Chauhan took the call. They wanted the highest-ranking officer to come out. As *Badé Sahib*[3] is out of station, you were the only one I could think of calling."

She could visualise the reluctance that must have gone into placing that call. As the first female API in Shimla, she was used to being treated as a bit of fluff. It only made her more determined. Some said pugnacious, but that was their problem.

The lights were blazing in the Big Bangla. It could be spotted five miles away, placed as it was on a hill. The approach was treacherous at the best of times, but at 4am, on icy roads, it was a hellish drive. She gripped her seat as Narinder peered ahead in the darkness, uttering muffled oaths every time the tyres slipped.

"What can be so urgent, that they couldn't wait for a more decent hour?" She wondered aloud.

"No one says no to the Minister, *Sahib*.[4] You had better get used to it."

She wondered if he knew of her history and why she had been posted here. Then she figured, probably not. It was just a comradely heads-up for her. She didn't bother replying.

The gates loomed up quite suddenly, and Narinder had to brake hard, sending the jeep spinning slightly to the left.

"*Kaun hai*[5]?" the chowkidar came running out, his blanket covering his head, the stick banging threateningly against the bonnet.

"Police!" cried out Narinder, suppressing the tremor in his voice.

The gates were opened once their identities were verified. The drive leading to the house was clear of all snow, and in the dark she could make out vague shapes of the caretaker's house and tenements of the other servants the Minister employed.

The servants all stood together in a huddle outside the main entrance. From inside she could hear an occasional bellow.

"*Saare chutiye hain*[6]! All bloody useless bastards!" The cuss words kept getting more colourful, even as she took the steps two at a time.

"Minister *ji*[7]?" She addressed the back of the tall man who was pacing the floor. He turned to stare at her.

"Who are you? Where is Brijesh?"

"I am sorry but the DCP is away in Delhi. He is not expected back till the end of the month. I am ACI Soumitra Ghosh. Recently posted here, sir. How can I help?"

"How..." He spluttered. "You...? I need a man to handle this case. Not you. Send someone else!"

"At this hour of the morning, you get me, or no one at all. Now, what seems to be the problem?"

His mouth opened and closed for what seemed like a minute. She assessed him quickly in the meantime. Tall, florid, moustached, several rings on his fingers, hair colour that came out of a bottle, and very expensive Italian shoes. Hmmm.

Silently he turned and walked towards a hallway. She was expected to follow, and she did, with Narinder at her heel. She barely glanced at the various portraits that adorned the walls, instead trying to sneak a peek through the few open doorways and the shadowy rooms beyond.

He entered a large bedroom. The room was charmingly under-stated, its muted pistachio and blush colour scheme indicating a woman's tasteful touch. The bed was made, the curtains were drawn. The air was heavy with an exotic perfume mingled with a faint metallic odour. Then she spotted it. The leg that stuck out innocuously from behind the bed.

He stood back watching her response. She walked slowly around to the other side of the bed. Her intake of breath was involuntary. The body lay at an unnatural angle. Half under the bed, half out. The throat had been viciously slit. There were puncture wounds all over the torso. Copious amounts of blood had soaked through the pale blue nightie and into the Persian rug underneath. A bottle of 'Samsara' lay smashed next to the body.

"My wife."

"When did you find her?"

"An hour ago, when I came home."

"Has anything been touched in this room?"

"No...nothing. I called the station right away."

She looked over to Narinder who stood gaping at the body. It was probably the first dead body he had seen in his career.

"Call Rao. Tell him to get here straight away."

She looked at the impassive face of the Minister. "Can you think of anyone who could be responsible for this?"

He looked at her blankly. "I have many enemies. But Tabassum? No. Everyone loved her. Even the servants."

"Your wife was Muslim?" She'd gathered as much from the name.

"Kashmiri. Yes, Kashmiri Muslim. But non-practising." As if that mattered.

"Minister *ji*...I need to seal this room off till our Forensics man arrives. But first, I need to look around."

"Be my guest." He sat heavily in the chair near the door.

With a flick of her head, she posted Narinder as a guard, and started her reconnaissance of the room. The windows were all locked, and the one door that led into the garden was barred with iron grills, allowing no entry or egress. She let the curtain drop noting the heavy damask material that had to be imported. Turning to the dresser she observed a variety of perfumes, mostly from the house of Guerlain. She looked at the bottles with their exotic names- '*Chant d'Aromes*', '*Idylle*', '*Jardins de Bagatelle*'. One empty spot. Perhaps that's where '*Samsara*' had come from. No makeup except for *kajal*[8]. She looked at the photos on the dresser, and realised that this was a woman who had never needed the artifice of cosmetics. Her beauty was a natural albeit almost an otherworldly one. An Indian Ingrid Bergman, with wide spaced grey eyes, wavy jet-black hair, and a dewiness that only the very fortunate were blessed with. She also looked considerably younger than her husband.

"How old was your wife?"

"Forty two...no...forty three. She'd just turned forty three."

The Minister was easily in his late fifties.

"Any children?"

"Three boys, all at boarding school. Look Mrs Ghosh..."

"Miss."

"What? Okay. Miss Ghosh, I am exhausted. It's been a long day, and this..." He waved his hands about. "This has been a shock. How much longer?"

She examined his face and saw no trace of any emotion. Perhaps as a seasoned politician he was used to hiding his feelings. But it was decidedly odd.

"I understand Minister *ji*." She injected a dose of compassion in her voice. "And please call me Soumi." She wanted him on her side for now.

Pale morning light was starting to filter through the gaps in the curtains.

"I can finish up in here. My team will be arriving shortly. Please try and get some rest. I will be needing your help later, with some enquiries and also to question your staff."

"Yes, thank you Soumi." He suddenly sounded weary. "Please... uhhh...let me know when you...uhhh...remove her body. I want to be there."

She ushered him out, and then turned to look at a silent Narinder.

"Post a guard outside his room, and call the Telephone Exchange. I want all phone calls monitored."

"Sahib, how can we do that? If he finds out..."

"I don't care. This is a murder investigation, and he is the prime suspect."

TWO WEEKS HAD FLOWN BY, and she was no closer to a resolution. The murder had become national headlines, with every newspaper screaming outrage and conspiracies. All sorts of theories had been bandied about, and if it wasn't for the fact that her superior had broken his leg, and was currently immobile in Delhi, she would have been off the case. She had already been called incompetent, worthless, a bimbo and far worse by the Press and by the Minister's camp. To add insult to injury, her mother had decided to visit from Kolkata.

"Maa, you could not have chosen a worse time!"

"What kind of a daughter does not welcome her mother to her house?"

"Oh Maa! Just look at you. You have three sweaters, a shawl, and four pairs of socks on, and you're still shivering. Why are you here in December? You are not used to these temperatures. Why didn't you come in May, like I'd said?"

"Soumi...you need to get married."

"Huh?"

"I have seen a very good boy. I wanted to talk to you about him."

"No! Maa, I am in the middle of a very serious case. I am not having this conversation again."

With that, she grabbed her briefcase and stomped out of the house.

Walking up the steep hill, she mulled over the details of the case in her mind.

Rao had established the time of death as somewhere between 1am and 2am. There had been no forced entry. There were no signs of a struggle. The assailant must have been known to the victim.

The Minister's alibi had been watertight. He had indeed been in a meeting with several other members of his department. The meeting had overrun, and alcohol and kebabs had been involved. This ruled him out, but only just.

The shell-shocked servants had been unable to provide any answers. The chowkidar had only registered the tailor who had come to deliver Madam's newly stitched blouses. That was at 5pm. But he had left three quarters of an hour later.

Nothing had been disrupted. Nothing had ostensibly been stolen either. No obvious motive. Yet, the brutality of the attack indicated a crime of passion.

Hmmm.

She sat down on a bench on the Mall Road. The early risers were about, mingling with the honeymooning couples. She watched as a young groom got his pretty wife to sit and pose on a horse, making sure she displayed her gaudy wedding jewellery, while he took the obligatory love-struck photos. How long before this love soured? How long before she became another pudding-faced, plump, baby factory and he, the wife beating, whiskey-swilling lout? She gave it five years.

She turned to look at the snowcapped peaks of the Himalayas. Their majestic beauty never failed to awe her. This - this was real. This had existed before, and it would exist much after their own silly little lives had come to an end.

"*Sahib ji*?" A quiet, nervous voice whispered next to her.

Startled, she looked up at the slight young girl who stood by her, shuffling from one foot to another.

"*Sahib ji*, I wanted to talk to you about Madam. Tabassum madam."

"Yes? What about her?" She asked, impatient to be on her way. She had heard enough of Tabassum's good deeds, of how wonderful she had been with the servants, how charitable with the poor, how generous with her time. How her beauty had been far more than just skin deep. There was just one problem with the picture. It didn't factor in a motive for the grisly murder.

"I'm Gulabo. My father is the estate gardener but we don't live on the estate."

Soumi stood up. "Walk with me."

Gulabo tried keeping pace with her strides.

"Tabassum madam was teaching me English. She said I was smart. That I shouldn't have stopped school. But Baba didn't want me to study any further. He said I was to be married in a few years, and too much education would give me unsuitable ideas."

"Madam would come once a week. I looked forward to those lessons..." She said wistfully. "She would bring me presents sometimes. Little trinkets. Old salwar suits that I could alter to wear."

"Two weeks ago..." She hesitated.

Sensing a break, Soumi stopped and looked her square in the face.

"Yes? What happened two weeks ago?"

"Madam was late. I thought she wasn't coming. When she did, she seemed very upset. Distracted. She kept losing track of what she was saying... That same night...she was killed." The girl started to sob.

"There, there." Soumi patted her absently. So, something had happened. Something that had upset the perfect Tabassum. What could it be?

AT THE STATION, she summoned Narinder. "I thought we were interviewing the tailor today. Is he back from his sister's wedding?"

"Yes *Sahib*. He has been waiting for you. Shall I bring him in?"

Rajinder Prasad aka Raju had a nervous twitch and a squint. Soumi found it disconcerting and chose to peruse her file instead.

"What time did you go to madam's house?"

"Around 5pm *Sahib*."

"What had you made for her?'

"Some blouses *Sahib*. New design. Backless, with string."

"Backless? Did Tabassum madam wear these sorts of blouses often?"

Raju's twitch became more pronounced. "No *Sahib*. She never...I mean...mostly her blouses were normal... But this time she brought photo. Some *fillum*[9] star lady. Said she wanted same to same."

"She asked you to copy the design?"

"Yes *Sahib*."

"Did she say where she would wear this to?"

"No *Sahib*. Madam did not talk about those things with me."

"Okay. You can go."

The weapon had never been found. From the trajectory of the cut, Rao had deduced it to be a *khukri*, a Nepalese carved knife. This wasn't a particularly outstanding piece of information, as plenty of Nepalese immigrants populated Shimla, working as porters, guards and in the apple orchards. The Minister had had no Nepalese servants, however. What was even more of a worry was, that if the crime had indeed been committed by a Nepalese, then he (or she) could be well over the border in Nepal by now. The extradition treaty between India and Nepal was an old and tenuous one and did not provide enough leverage to seek any kind of redress, once the criminal had fled the country.

"I need to speak with the Minister again."

"Is that wise? I mean...He was not happy about the Telephone exchange business."

"My problem. Go get the jeep."

Narinder was quiet the entire journey. She could sense that he was bristling at being outranked and ordered about. Yet, a begrudging respect had started to creep into their exchanges. She decided to return the favour.

"What do you think Narinder? You have lived here all your life. You've known these people. Who could have done this? And why?"

"I don't *know* these people Sahib. I know *of* them."

"Yes...whatever... But no ideas? No guesses?"

He gave her a quick, assessing glance before turning his attention back to the road. "One hears things. The Minister's hands are not clean. He has held on to his post at all costs. Maybe he paid too high a price?"

A hush seemed to have descended on the Big Bangla. It had been the site of frenzied activity the last few weeks. From sniffer dogs to investigative teams, from mourners, to relatives to friends, people had trooped in and out with scant regard. Yet, today, it seemed to stand forlorn. As though its very heart had been ripped out. She shook her head to clear it of these fanciful meanderings.

The chowkidar let them in with barely a glance. As they turned on the drive, she once again observed the beauty of the grounds. This had been a sensuous woman who liked to surround herself with pulchritude. Everything in her life had a grace, a refinement, a charm and a delicacy. Who would want to annihilate that?

The Minister was in no mood to receive them.

"We will wait here." Soumi said to the maid.

"Bring some *chai*[10]." Narinder commanded. She caught his eye and grinned.

They sat themselves down, prepared for a long wait.

"So you are the Bengali inspector." A voice drawled from the doorway. She looked up, and her breath caught in her throat. The most beautiful specimen of masculinity stood in front of her. His frame was whippet thin but did not conceal the patrician musculature. He had his father's height, but his mother's grey eyes and dark, wavy hair. If he was aware of his effect on the opposite sex, it did not much bother him. He looked at her up and down. She stood up, suddenly feeling very small and helpless.

"Yes, I am API Ghosh." She wanted a formality there. A distance.

"I'm Ken. Kamran actually. But everyone calls me Ken. You can too."

He leaned over and picked a thread off her cardigan. She swallowed hard. Why was this eighteen-year-old having this effect on her? It was ridiculous. She cleared her throat. "How long will your father be? We have other things to do as well."

His eyes flashed. "Such as? A petty theft or a carjacking? What could be more important than my *Ammi's* murder investigation?"

"Yes, what could indeed? Please ask your father to join us so that we may proceed with our enquiries."

Two younger boys came running in, cheeks flushed, breathing hard from the exertion. They looked in their early teens, and although neither possessed the same breathtaking good looks, they were a pair of healthy, robust lads messing about. The only thing that belied this was the purple tinge around their eyes. Tears and sleepless nights. The legacy of the living.

"We are on special leave, for the funeral." Ken supplied the information carelessly. He sat opposite her, his gaze never leaving her face.

"Are you really as incompetent as they say?"

"That depends on who says it..."

"*Sahib* is a very good policewoman. You should not go by hearsay." She was surprised at Narinder's sudden support and smiled at him.

"I see. Then, tell me API Ghosh - who killed my mother and why?"

"As you are aware, Ken, we are still investigating...There are things I need to know. Friends I need to interview. Your father has denied me access to her papers. Unless I have every piece of the puzzle, I can't determine whether this was a random attack, or whether, as we suspect, a specific, targeted one."

"My mother...*Ammi*[11]..." He looked at Narinder, who looked down. "She was a beautiful woman. A pure and pious soul. For the longest time, it was just her and I. The two of us, battling against the world. Till Raj came along and swept her off her feet." He laughed sardonically.

Soumi digested this information silently. She felt like a fool. No one had bothered to inform her that this was Tabassum's second marriage. How much more had been withheld from her?

"And your father... your biological one?"

"Gone...Dead...who cares? Never knew him."

The Minister walked in, his face like thunder.

"Ken, take your brothers inside. I will deal with this."

Ken unfolded himself languidly, and then with a quick wink escorted the boys out.

"You are snooping and prying again, Soumi! Instead of looking for the murderer, you keep trying to unearth God knows what in my household?! I am tired of this. I have been speaking to my contact in Delhi. They are sending a replacement. Better pull up your socks and start working hard. You are not going to last long."

"I need to look through Tabassum's personal effects."

"No!"

"You cannot keep denying me access..."

"I *cannot*?" He came right up to her. She could see the yellow in his eyes, smell his rancid breath, see the white roots of his jet-black hair. "My dear girl, this is India. I can do whatever I like. You are a nobody. You cannot stop me."

"What are you hiding Minister *ji*? If you really want her murder

solved, you would let me. There might be a clue in there. A letter...
something...anything..."

"And you think I haven't looked? I have searched high and low.
I've hunted for any small indication or tip. There is nothing!
Tabassum lived a transparent life. She had no secrets."

"Everyone has secrets, Minister *ji*. You should know that."

AFTER A FRUSTRATING DAY, returning to her mother's cooking
brought some respite. Tea and buttered toast had lost its allure some
months ago.

"You have gotten so thin Soumi..." Her mother fussed around her.
"Always rushing about. Not enough sleep. Not enough food. Where is
the sense in this life?"

"I enjoy it Maa. It's what I do. I am good at it too." She remembered her old trainer's words. That she had the instincts of a blood-
hound. Her instincts were telling her that something didn't add up.

"Tell me, Maa, is anyone ever really good? I mean, completely,
thoroughly good?"

Her mother laughed. "Soumi, I thought you'd given up reading
fairy tales in kindergarten."

She laughed alongside. Cynicism was a trait she had obviously
inherited.

"WELL, I only agreed to meet you because Ken called and insisted,"
said the elegant Naureen, who sat sipping her coffee ever so daintily.
"What do you want to know?"

"Tell me about Tabassum. All that you know. Even the most irrel-
evant detail."

The diamonds in her ears glinted as she cocked her head to a side
and looked at Soumi speculatively.

"She would have liked you. She respected intelligent women.
Gutsy women. Women who'd stepped into male domains." She
sighed. "What a lot of people didn't know about Tabassum was that

she was a very bright woman herself. A topper in school and college. Desperate to do something with her qualifications. But her father married her off to that useless Farroukh. Then Kamran was born, and all her ambitions withered and died."

"What happened to Farroukh?"

"You don't know?" She seemed surprised. "He was killed by the insurgents in Kashmir. Kamran was only two. Tabassum left Srinagar and moved to Delhi with him. That's where she met Raj."

"Why does Ken hate his father?"

"Which one?" She laughed. "Kamran has always been possessive about Tabassum. He was only a baby but some impressions of his biological father's abuse must have survived in his subconscious. As for Raj, he doesn't hate him, he just tolerates him. No man was ever good enough for her, not in Kamran's opinion."

"Who do you think did this?"

"I don't know. I am equally baffled. I have known Tabassum for over thirty years, and in all honesty, she was the loveliest person. Not a wicked bone in her body." A tear rolled down her face, and she wiped it discreetly with her lace edged handkerchief.

"Are there any other friends I should speak to? Anyone else who was close to her?"

"Most everyone is either in Chandigarh for the Winter or holidaying abroad. There is that Dolly, of course." Her little *moué* conveyed distaste and annoyance.

"Dolly?"

"Some upstart who'd attached herself to Tabassum this past year."

"Where can I find her?"

"Probably at some kitty party or another. She is one of those insufferably loquacious people, always surrounded by a gaggle. What Tabassum ever saw in her, I cannot begin to fathom!"

"*SAHIB*, you have till the end of this week. Then, the new inspector arrives to take over the case."

"Yes, Narinder, I am aware of that." She spooned the lukewarm *sambar* [12]into her mouth. "Where did you buy this crap from?"

"There is a new South Indian restaurant *Sahib*. I know one of the waiters."

"This tastes nothing like *idli*[13], and the *sambar*[14] is like water. Tell your friend the chef better get his act together, or I'll be paying him a visit," she mock threatened. "And what of this Dolly Kalra? Have you located her yet?"

"*Sahib*, you think I do nothing but drink *chai*? She has a shop on the Mall. Kalra's. They sell shawls and stoles. Some other woollen things too."

"Narinder, I don't need an inventory!" She swallowed the last morsel of whatever was masquerading as food. "Let's go pay her a visit."

KALRA'S: The board screamed in neon lettering. There was nothing subtle or nuanced here. Inside, the shop was brightly lit. The wares displayed in a surprisingly ordered manner. The cheaper shawls were hung up for inspection, and random touching. The more expensive were kept under the glass, to be displayed only upon request.

Dolly was hard to miss. Her yellow salwar suit clung to her curves, ample as they were. The neckline was plunging, and the scarf a mere accessory to the fact, slung over her shoulders not to camouflage but to emphasise.

A portly man with hennaed hair and matching teeth sat behind the cash counter, rapidly counting the wad of Rupees he held.

"Hello *ji*. Namaste *ji*." She came over to them, all dimples and smiles.

An hour later the smiles had all but disappeared. Her sodden handkerchief was a testament to her grief. Her dear, dear friend had been so viciously killed.

"I never saw you at the funeral?" Soumi asked, the histrionics wearing thin on her.

"Oh! I wanted to come. So much. But my husband said perhaps it was not a good time."

"Why not?" She glanced over to the hennaed Mr Dolly who sat like a stone Buddha watching them question his wife at the back of his store.

"Well, we are not...the same class. The other people did not like our friendship. Tabassum was like a sister to me. Others were jealous of this."

"How did the two of you meet?" She could not imagine them crossing paths socially.

"Oh!" she simpered, her dimples playing on her cheeks. "She came in one day to buy a shawl. She seemed lonely. We got chatting and that was it." She finished triumphantly, as though her winsome personality won her friends on a regular basis.

"How often did you meet?"

"Daily."

"Daily? When? What did you do?"

"We would meet for lunch. Go for walks. Go to the library. Just hang out."

"Hang out?" observed Soumi wryly.

"BRING HER IN." She rasped to Narinder on the phone. Her throat felt like razor blades were scraping the inside of it. She looked at the pile of soggy, mucus-soaked tissues near her bed, and looked away. Her mother came in, brandishing the thermometer like a sword.

"Not now, Maa," she groaned, "I am in the middle of something."

"I don't care. Open your mouth."

"Gaaahhhh. Aaaahhhh."

"*Sahib*? *Sahib*, are you okay?"

"Yes, Narinder," she spluttered, spitting out the thermometer. "I am coming to the station in an hour. Get that Dolly in. I need to question her, without the husband around."

"You are going nowhere Miss. Not in your condition."

"Oh Maa. It's only a bit of fever. I need to go. I am this close to a breakthrough. I can feel it in my bones."

"Go then." Her mother said, quietly. "When did you ever listen to me? You were always your father's daughter. After him, I ceased to matter."

"Maa...that is not true!" She cried. "How can you even say that? Look...listen...let me go. I promise, when I return, we'll have a serious talk about this Professor chap you want me to meet. Okay? There, that's better. Love you Maa."

She grabbed her coat and ran out before her mother's mood changed again.

DOLLY HAD dark circles under her eyes. She squirmed uncomfortably in the chair.

"I need to get back soon. My husband..."

"Someone will inform your husband you are here. Don't worry."

"Now, tell me more about this room you have on hire at Prospect Hill. I understand that you have paid upfront for it. For what... ummm...let's see...another six months?"

"Yes...yes...I, uhhh, I go there to write."

"Write? What do you write?"

"Some poetry. Urdu *Shayyari*[15]. Tabassum was helping me. Her Urdu was so chaste."

"Then I presume you have some of these writings with you?"

"No...I store them on my laptop."

"A laptop? I didn't realise you were so tech savvy?"

At this, she raised her chin and said proudly, "I did Computer Science at school!"

"Very impressive. So, where is this laptop stashed?"

"It's...uhhh...it crashed a week ago. I need to get it repaired."

"Crashed? As in, all the programs crashed?"

"No...it..uhhh...slipped out of my hands. It fell. It's broken."

"Oh, that's unfortunate. As luck would have it, I know an excellent repair guy. Why don't you let Narinder bring it back here? We can have it fixed and also look at some of those poems, hmmm? Hard drives are amazingly resilient things. All sorts of data can be retrieved from them, despite any damage to the computer. But I'm sure you know that. You studied Computer Science, after all."

"Why are you questioning me like this?" Dolly jumped up. "I have done nothing wrong!"

"Sit down." The menace in her voice was unmistakable now. "Why don't you stop lying to me at once, and tell me exactly what was going on in that room? Why, every afternoon, while your husband took his afternoon siesta, you and Tabassum would take yourselves off, for hours at a time? What did you do? Tell me!"

Dolly started to shake uncontrollably. Narinder brought over a cup of sweetened *chai*. She could barely hold the cup in her trembling hands.

"At first, we just watched." She whispered.

"Watched? Watched what?"

"Porn. Young men. With other women. With men. Then…"

"Then what…?"

"You have to understand. We were both young women married to old men. There was no sex in our lives. Our husbands…they were too busy to give us that…"

"Then what happened? Did you try it on one another?"

Narinder cleared his throat. "*Sahib*, shall I go?"

"No. Stay. I need this recorded."

Two red spots burnt high on her cheeks. "We were not like that."

"So, then?"

"She wanted men. She wanted me to get her men. Young men. No older than twenty she said. She was willing to pay for it."

"So, you became her procurer?" A fit of coughing assailed her then. Narinder rushed to get her a glass of water. "What did you get in return? Her scraps? Did you share? Did you take it in turns?"

"You…you are making it sound so cheap…so sick…"

"Because, Dolly *ji*, it is! It is cheap and sick to buy services of boys young enough to be your sons!"

Dolly's eyes filled with tears and she looked away.

"What happened on the day of the murder? Something happened. She was scared and worried."

"There was one boy. We had used him before. We liked him. He started to get obsessive. Threatened to tell."

"Did he know who you were? Who she was?"

"He must have figured it out. Perhaps seen a photo in the newspaper. I don't know. He was blackmailing her."

"Who was this boy? What was his name? How did you contact him?"

THE SITE WAS EASILY accessible to anyone who knew how. Soumi wished she could unlearn this information. What she saw made her sick to the stomach. Boys as young as eight, posed provocatively, sexually, offering their bodies as commodities to be used and abused. Dolly had led them to the link that offered the services of boys ranging from fourteen to nineteen. Tabassum's preference lay in this range. In vain they hunted for the boy called Rohan.

"Start again. Go slowly. We need to examine these carefully."

"No...none of these... He must have taken himself off... I don't know...He... No! Wait...wait... Go back... there's something about this one..."

The face was in profile, shadowed, but his body shone, well oiled, the six-pack taking centre stage.

"Make a booking."

"What? Me? I...?"

"Yes, you. Book him. Call him this afternoon."

With the honey trap laid, they waited for him to arrive. When he did, Soumi's heart plummeted. She looked over at Narinder, whose eyes were nearly popping out of their sockets. The resemblance was uncanny. Was Ken Rohan? Or was Rohan a mere lookalike?

He sauntered through the lobby of the inn, briefly pausing to look at a magazine. Then he took the stairs to the room.

When they burst in ten minutes later, he was stepping out of his jeans.

"Police!"

Narinder had tackled him to the floor and managed to get a pair of handcuffs on him. Soumi was relieved to discover it was not Ken. His features were flatter. His eyes a murky brown. He was shorter and had the distinctive down turn to his eyes that the Nepalese did.

"It's him." Dolly shuddered. "He was blackmailing her."

"So, what did you do with the murder weapon Rohan? Where did you hide it?"

"What...what are you talking about? I didn't kill her. Why would I? She was my cash cow. My golden goose." He laughed suddenly. "She was good in bed too."

"Shut up!" screamed Dolly. "You did it. I know you did it! After all she gave you. All she did for you..."

"Did for me? I was just a son substitute. Ken was the star of the show all along."

At this Dolly fell silent.

"What do you mean?" prodded Soumi. "How do you know Ken?"

HE LOUNGED on the sofa in front of her.

"Not so incompetent then API Ghosh."

"No."

"Who will believe you? You have no evidence. No murder weapon. Nothing except the salacious words of a gigolo."

"A childhood friend of yours Ken."

"Rohan dropped out of school years ago. Got mixed up in a bad crowd...drugs, petty crime. I lost touch with him."

"Yes, you did. Till recently when he contacted you. Telling you how he was screwing your mother." She leaned forward. "How did that make you feel Ken? A bit impotent? Full of rage? Here was *another* man, replacing you in her life. You wanted to be the only man, didn't you? You wanted her for yourself. All of her. Always had."

"Shut up bitch!" His spittle landed on her face. "You don't know anything."

"I know enough to know that yours was an unnatural relationship. Perhaps the Minister sensed it? So he sent you away to boarding school. But it didn't die, did it?"

She stood up and circled him.

"I have witnesses who saw you board the bus the morning after the murder. Your friends at school have told me how you disappeared for two days. We have retrieved the email Rohan sent you, along with the photo of him and Tabassum. Confess now, and I might be able to plead clemency for you."

She watched him crumple on to the floor, his howl renting the air with its agony.

"THEY CANCELLED THE REPLACEMENT *SAHIB*." Narinder tucked into his *dosa* [16]with relish.

"Well, there was hardly any point, was there?" The *sambar* had definitely improved in consistency, if not in taste.

"Such a scandal! They found the *khukri*[17] in his school locker."

"Hmmm." She stayed impassive.

"I hear they are treating him at some asylum. He has gone quite mad."

"Narinder, tell the chef he needs to buy some spicy gun powder... the eating kind..." She looked at his perplexed face and laughed. "Never mind. Tell him to work on the *sambar* first."

They walked back to the station in convivial silence, the mountains quiet spectators to their budding friendship.

3

CREEP

He sidled up to her, crab like in his approach. His shirt was stretched tight over his pot belly, buttons threatening to detonate any moment.

"Hello," he smiled greasily, "Why is your glass empty? A beautiful lady like you should never have an empty glass."

She smiled vaguely in his direction and allowed him to bring her a refill. It was his lucky day. He was sure of it. The goddess of his dreams stood in front of him, in the flesh. He wondered if she knew how many fantasies she'd spawned, how many nightfalls she had triggered. Admittedly she was a lot larger now than she had been back then, but she'd filled out in the right places. His eyes lingered on her ample bosom. He licked his lips inadvertently.

"You may not remember me, but I was in the same school as you."

"Oh, were you?" Her eyes flickered a modicum of interest.

"Yes, yes. One year junior. But heh heh. I was quite thin and lanky back then."

"I don't remember you, I'm sorry. I was only in that school for a couple of years."

"Yes, but you see, I could never forget you. So beautiful back then. Even more beautiful now."

She smiled sadly and twirled the lime in her glass.

"Come, let's sit down." He let his hand rest on the small of her back, guiding her over to a secluded corner. "I want to know all about you. What you have been doing for the past twenty years. Where you have been. I'm sure it's an exciting story..."

An hour later, he was bored senseless. The talk had veered from her life to his, her spouse to his, her kids to his, till it had shot off into new age mumbo jumbo category. For the first time, her eyes had lit up. Animated, she had thrown theories of ghosts, aliens, seances and retreats at him. Flinching inwardly at the vain stupidity of it all, outwardly he had agreed, nodding and smiling, and leaning in, as close as she would allow. He'd watched her lips move, imagining all that he would do to that mouth, disregarding the prattle, his mind just about controlling the loins from declaring themselves.

Finally, she paused for breath and looked at him.

"So, what brings you here?"

"I try and come once every few years. It's a good way to catch up with old mates. I've made loads of LinkedIn connections here. In my business, I make it my business to network."

He smiled. Then he boldly reached forward and stroked her inner wrist. "Today, I feel like I have made the most important connection of my life."

She giggled and pulled away. "I'm a married woman!"

"So what? You are just a woman today - a very beautiful one. You deserve to be loved, every delicious inch of you. Love is the most divine connection of them all. Don't you think?"

He watched her pupils dilate in surprise, and then she blushed.

Bingo! He kept a sweet, patient smile on his face, but once again took to rubbing his thumb sensuously across her wrist.

"Samira... Samira... there you are! I've been looking everywhere... Oh!" A plump, officious looking woman came barrelling towards them. She stopped short, noting their closeness.

His goddess jumped up, all flustered.

"I'm sorry... I ran into an old friend. This is ——..." She looked confused.

He could not believe that the entire evening was coming to naught. He tried salvaging it.

"Well, could I take you out to dinner Samira? Still so much to catch up on."

"No, I think I'd better go. Thank you for a lovely evening. Look me up on LinkedIn."

She wafted away with the interfering so-and-so.

He slumped down, deflated. One button finally gave up the ghost and popped, rolling away forlornly. What bloody luck! Just when he had learned how to inveigle himself into women's affections, just when he had seen how far flattery could get you, just when he thought he'd hit the jackpot, bad luck had intervened again. He pulled out his wallet and looked at the picture of his plump, smiling wife, and his plump, smiling children and sighed. He wanted to swim with the swans. Instead, he had to waddle with the ducks.

He drank his whiskey in one gulp and stood up, mentally writing off the evening. He was in no mood to network now. The hotel bed and the porn channel called out to him. He started to shuffle towards the exit.

Then he spotted her. He was sure it was her. She had lived next door for a few years till her family moved away. She was a few years younger and only just starting to develop back then. He used to switch off the lights in his room and watch her change out of his binoculars.

He sidled up to her, smiling greasily.

"Deepa, it is you, isn't it?"

4

MA VIE SANS COULEUR

BLUE (cerulean, sapphire, indigo, cyan):
The colour of the ocean, or the sky, or even better, the deep, dark, mysterious blue of the sapphire that hangs on her mother's neck.

She dabs a bit of blue on the brush, and with sure, swift strokes, deposits it on the canvas before her. It is dark, rich and pigmented in the centre, till she swirls it out, and the colour spreads thickly, rapidly reaching out to the edges, as though seeking to escape the confines of its parameters.

Her finger touches the blue. She feels the tackiness of it. Smells the faint metallic odour.

"Sophie?"

"Hmmm?"

"No, it is not enough. You have to be one with the canvas. You have to be the creator, and the creation."

She looks up at the large figure of her father. Hears his raspy breath as he points and gesticulates, the smoke from his cigar billowing up around him.

Her heart swells with adoration.

Thump. Thump. Thump.

It is her again. Thumping her stick on the floor.

"Sophie? Sophieeeeeee!"

"Coming! I'm coming…"

YELLOW (LEMON, amber, canary, citrine):

The sun is setting outside, and her studio has an otherworldly glow about it. Briefly she wonders whether there is any point in trying to capture the sunset. Then she turns and appraises herself in the mirror. Not today.

Her dress has yellow daffodils on it. They make her happy. A little gloss on her lips and she feels ready: a bit sexy, a bit daring.

"You look like an Anglo Indian." The old woman rocks back and forth in her chair, her lip curled, her eyes vicious.

She ignores her and takes the keys from the dresser.

Colin is late. She paces up and down under the watchful gaze of the crone.

An hour later, she knows he is not coming. She throws the keys to one side and dashes up the stairs.

There is still enough light to work. The paint falls in splodges on her dress. The yellow calms her down.

Lying in the sun. Kissing softly. One hand on her breast. The other reaching under her skirt. Pushing it away but laughing all the same.

Stretching out and feeling the rays on her face. Turning to him and running her hands down the length of his body, then suddenly changing her mind.

"Yes, yes, yes."

GREEN (VIRIDESCENT, sage, avocado, emerald):

The *maali* [1] is cutting the grass today. She can smell the freshness of it. The sonorous sound of the lawnmower at work is making her sleepy. She lies on the couch, half dozing. Her thighs are wet. She cannot understand why. She looks for her mother. Her mother is sitting at the piano, playing her favourite, Für Elise.

"*Maman? Maman?*"

She keeps playing, a sweet smile hovering on her lips, her head swaying to the music.

"*Maman?*"

She turns. Her eyes are blazing. She points at her skirt and screams "*Putain!*"

She awakes with a start. There is a dull pounding behind her eyes.

The soup she makes is enough for the two of them. They eat in silence.

"So, he didn't call?"

"No, *Maman*, he didn't."

"Another one that got away, eh Sophie? You will be an old maid like your auntie Renée." She cackles into her soup.

PINK (ROSE, salmon, coral, fuchsia):

The roses arrive two days later. There is a small card with a 'sorry' written on it. She doesn't know what to make of it.

She takes them into her room and deposits them in a vase. They are pink, overblown, fantastically sensuous. Their heady fragrance repels her. She watches them from a distance. She takes one and crushes the petals between her fingers, till the scent is all over her hand. She smears it on her face. Not enough. Never enough.

They are kissing behind the curtain. She can hear them. She peeks. Her father sits with his thighs splayed. Renée sits on him. Up and down they bounce. She watches, fascinated. Renée's pink tongue protrudes, and she sighs, a deep long sigh. They shudder in unison. She replaces the curtain and runs quietly back to her room.

GREY (STORM, slate, dove, clay):

The ocean is a deep, murky grey that mimics her mood. She walks alone on the beach. It is early morning and the hawkers are setting up their stalls. They ignore her as she drifts past. They stopped paying attention a long time ago.

She watches the child collect shells. He is small but wiry. His limbs are browned from the sun, and suddenly she is envious of his colour, his brownness, his earthiness.

"They are a dirty people. Uncivilised, uncouth, unclean. They need to be ruled with a firm hand. Our forefathers did a lot of good in this country. Look, what we've made of this sorry patch of land! Look at what they have done since Independence. I tell you, Sophie, they are no good for themselves."

"But Maman..."

"But nothing! Someday you will visit France and see... You will understand..."

<u>BROWN</u> (wood, **oak**, tan, ochre):

"Memsahib?"

"Yes, Ajay?"

"The groceries have arrived. Do you want to go over the bill?"

She peruses the familiar items, marking off the prices absent-mindedly, looking for the invariable few rupees that go missing along the way. She sees it and ignores it. **"Fool!"** *Maman* screams in her mind. She suppresses her sudden shiver.

"Put it all away Ajay and tell Rajan to buy some extra lamb for the stew tomorrow."

The newspaper headlines jostle with one another to be the most calamitous. She reads them briefly.

The bundle of Paris Match has been delivered to the old woman's room. She doesn't emerge till noon. Then, it seems as though she has been crying.

"If it weren't for your father dying so suddenly, I would have been home now. Who was to know he had so many debts? Now I will be stuck in this godforsaken country forever."

Brown against white. It makes a pretty contrast. They laugh about it. They are young, still. He touches her skin reverentially.

"You are the most beautiful creature I have ever made love to."

"And how many creatures have you made love to?" She giggles into his ear.

They kiss and hold each other tight, squeezing the breath out of each other's bodies, trying to amalgamate into one: Brown and White, White and Brown.

WHITE (ALMOND, **cream, lily, oyster**):

What was she looking for? She cannot remember. There are papers scattered everywhere. Only one paper matters. The one she is holding in her hand. Her mother's birth certificate.

She enters her room. It is close to dusk, and she is watching an old movie on the Television.

"Why did you lie to me?"

"*Comment?*" She turns to her impatiently, immediately noting the paper in her hand.

"You lied."

She watches her through half lidded eyes.

"Sophie, you are a fool! That piece of paper means nothing."

"To you... to you..." She sobs. "But to me...! All my life you said you were pure. That there was no mixed blood...but all along...this... this...your mother...?"

The old woman stands up with an effort, and comes towards her. The force of her slap sends her reeling backwards.

"Listen to me, you little wretch! I am French through and through. Do you understand?"

She is not allowed to say goodbye to him. She is shipped off to Paris. In that civilised world, she feels like an alien. There are no friends here, only strangers. Her art is all she has. She grows thin and develops a stoop. No one wants her now. She is so white she is almost transparent.

GOLD (AURELIAN, **gilt, flaxen, honey**):

It is at the Consulate General they meet again. So many years.

They have been kind to him. His eyes pass over her, only to return; shocked, bemused.

"How are you, Sophie?"

"I...I..." She stutters embarrassingly.

She cannot get enough of him. Her eyes travel over his widened girth, the grey at his temples, the thin scar above his lip.

"Meet my wife - Anjolie."

A burnt orange sari encases silken limbs. Her eyes are lined with kohl, and her gaze is not unkind. They float away together, in a golden haze.

Father Dead. Come home.

The mountain of debts paid off slowly by the sale of the family silver, the land and the cars. His paintings are worthless. Mediocre artist. There is no depth here, she is informed. She puts them away in an unused room. She cannot look at them anymore.

SILVER (CHROME, pewter, pearly, argent):

The cheque for her first sale arrives in the morning post. Rs 15,000. It will do. There is a buzz about her paintings now. One reviewer calls them 'full of rage and unexplained angst'. She laughs at that.

She looks through her drawer and finds the thin silver chain her father gave her on her sixteenth birthday. It is somewhat tarnished, but she wears it with pride, and something akin happiness.

She enters the room and opens the shutters. The paintings lie there propped against the wall. Slowly she pulls off the sheets and examines them again. They are curious things. She can see herself in so many - a foot here, a small hand there - all hers. She posed for them.

Then she looks at the last one he painted. The one she has not shown *Maman*.

Renée lying on her side, her breasts pendulous, her stomach rounded. One hand propping her up, one hand on the dark thatch between her legs.

She looks at it for a long time.

There is a small, dark eyed boy standing next to Renée. He shakes hands politely.

"Sophie, this is Jacques. My son."

She doesn't need to know anymore. She turns and flees, never to return to that apartment on the 11th Arrondissement.

BLACK (RAVEN, ebony, charcoal, night):

The old woman slurps her porridge noisily. She looks up suddenly. "Are you going out today? Where are you always disappearing to? You have no regard for me. I am always left behind."

"Come with me then."

"Come with you? Where? I cannot walk far...and in this heat?"

Sophie brings the cheque in.

"This needs depositing. I have to go to the bank."

The old woman inspects the cheque.

"Well, it is time you started to earn your keep. Go on...off you go. I will keep myself busy."

She returns late afternoon. The old woman is sitting in her rocking chair, careening back and forth with a manic intensity. There is a wild look in her eyes. She looks at Sophie and smirks.

Her father's paintings have been slashed.

Ripped.

Decimated.

She stands amidst the carnage, shaking.

"Sit still, little one. Papa must get the colour of your eyes just right. You have such pretty eyes, ma petite chou!"

"Papa, why don't you ever paint Maman?"

"Beauty such as your Maman's cannot be captured on canvas, Sophie."

RED (CARMINE, russet, cardinal, scarlet):

There are red spots before her eyes, and she cannot breathe. Memories lie in tatters about her. Slowly she starts gathering up the pieces of canvas she can salvage. She comes upon the knife that has wreaked the devastation. It lies mute, an instrument of a resurrected vendetta. She picks it up.

"Why *Maman*?"

The old woman rocks back and forth, her mouth twisting, her pupils dilated.

Sophie grabs the chair.

"Answer me!"

"His touch was filth. Everything...everything he touched turned dirty....Me...you... Renée...No more... No more filth..."

"Oh *Maman*!" She kneels at her feet, weeping. Gnarled fingers stroke her hair absently.

The blood is a deep, viscous red. There is so much of it. Who knew how much a human body contains? She lies in the velvet softness, letting its warmth seep through her weary limbs, the knife still held limply in her hand. The old woman's body lies slack in the chair.

"This won't hurt bébé. You are Papa's little poulette. Lie here. Let me show you how."

Her eyes start to close and slowly she drifts off to sleep. Her dreams are laced with crimson.

5

———

SECRETS AND LIES

Twenty six. Twenty seven. Twenty eight. My skipping rope flew through the air and under my feet in perfect arcs. Whoosh. Whoosh.

It was not the fact that he had died, it was how he had died. There were a lot of mutterings about it. It was clear enough though that concrete and skulls don't meet amicably. I thought he looked very peaceful as he lay there. I wanted to leave him there. Of course, they would have none of it.

"Should we call the police?" Malathi mumbled.

"I don't see why. It was an accident. He slipped and fell. There's no more to it." Bala answered.

"Let's call Doctor *Akka*[1]. She will know what to do."

Someone was promptly despatched.

Word must have spread. More and more people started to gather at the gates.

"What happened, child? Something happened, no? We heard Malathi scream."

I nodded nonchalantly and kept skipping. It was none of their business.

"Strange child that is, I tell you..." one whispered to the other. I ignored them. Fifty one. Fifty two. Fifty three.

Doctor *Akka* arrived ten minutes later and bustled in, stethoscope hanging loosely around her neck.

"He is dead." She pronounced this with grave solemnity. Malathi and Bala nodded in agreement. I could have told them that without a stethoscope.

All three looked down at him as he lay contentedly lifeless on the bedroom floor. Flies had started to buzz around him, attracted by the pool of blood under his head.

"Well," Doctor *Akka* sighed dramatically, "He was old, and his time had come. But what a shame. I always told him to ask for help. This would not have happened if he had. Such a proud man..." She sighed again. "I will sign the death certificate. Do you want to call the priest?"

Bala nodded. "Yes, I will. Only problem is that he wanted Damu to do his last rites."

"Damu?" She looked over at me. "But he is..."

"I know," Bala interjected quickly, "He can be coached."

Malathi wasn't convinced. "He rarely listens to us Bala." Then in an undertone. "He is a bit of a loose cannon, you know."

They stared at me.

Hundred and three. Hundred and four. Hundred and five.

"Call Rekha. He might be persuaded if she is here."

"I cannot abide the girl. Why must we have her under our roof again? Such a snake in the grass."

"Malathi, we cannot afford to be on our high horses right now. The quicker this is over, the sooner we can move on."

Doctor *Akka* looked at them quizzically.

"Perhaps, it is not my place, but a man has died in very unfortunate circumstances. What is it that you want 'over with' quickly?"

Malathi hastened to assure her. "Oh, don't get us wrong, Doctor *Akka*! We are so very upset. He had a good few years left in him. Of course, we are grief stricken. It's just that, well, we have to be practical. So much to be done. And with Damu, it is always so difficult."

"Yes, yes, I understand." She nodded. "So much to be done."

Hundred and thirty seven. Hundred and thirty eight. Hundred and thirty nine.

People came, people went. His body was moved. The floor was cleaned. He was bathed. Someone even shaved him. Then they laid him out in the courtyard, all wrapped up in a white sheet, with holy ash smeared on his forehead. The priest waddled in, followed by three assistants, who stared at me curiously.

"Don't mind the boy. He is like that only."

The priest looked offended but set about preparing all his *samagri*[2]. The coconut, the flowers, the vermillion, the incense sticks were all laid out in a particular order that fascinated me.

"Come here, Damu. Come and see." Malathi called to me quietly.

I was torn between getting to five hundred and investigating this curious ritual. At four hundred and sixty seven, I threw the rope aside and allowed myself to be lured to the spot.

FIVE HOURS EARLIER

"Damu... Damu?... Damu..!"

I relented enough to enter the old man's room.

"Damu," he said placatingly, "I know you are annoyed with me. But truly, I am not in any condition to play with you today."

I stood in the doorway.

"Come and sit by my side. I will tell you a story."

I stayed where I was.

"Come, boy. It is a good story and a true one."

I watched as his mouth moved. His lips were thin, and his stubble grey. I knew he had dimples when he smiled. He so rarely smiled these days. His eyes were a peculiar green that I had inherited.

"There was once a beautiful princess. She was loved and spoiled in equal measure. Anything she wanted, she could have. And she did have the best of it all... All except one thing..." He looked at me expectantly. I refused to take the bait. After a pause, he carried on. "That one thing was to be married to the man of her choosing. A peasant; a poor wretched man with no background to speak of. After all, she came from an illustrious pedigree. It would bring dishonour to the family - to her father's good name."

He fiddled with his watch.

"They ran away. She broke her poor father's heart. Slowly, he lost his riches and his will to live."

He looked at his shoes for a long time. I shuffled my feet impatiently. Then he looked up and smiled.

"His beloved queen nursed him back to health. They had another child, she reminded him. Together they rebuilt his kingdom and took care of the prince. The king lost a lot of his arrogance. He learnt humility and tolerance. Two virtues that are absolutely essential in one who has to lead."

He looked over at me.

"Does this story have a happy ending?" I asked.

"Well, that depends on a lot of things."

"What things?"

"Stories are somewhat linear, they begin somewhere and end somewhere. Life, on the other hand, is not a straight line. It is like a graph with many highs and many lows. If life finishes you off at a low, then it is a sad ending. If the full stop comes at a high, then it is a happy ending."

I was bored now, and wandered off, leaving him to cough and splutter blood into his handkerchief.

"COME ON DEAR, it is only a quick wash. You cannot perform the *puja*[3] without it."

Rekha held me firm. I thought of biting her arm, then thought better of it. I liked her. I let myself be led to the bathroom and given a bath. The soap smelled of him - of the old man. I supposed I would never smell sandalwood again without thinking of him.

Outside in the courtyard, people had gathered. Humming, buzzing, droning, they were like a swarm of bees. They scared me. Rekha allowed me to cling to her sari *pallav*[4].

"Come on Damu. The prayers have to start. You must listen carefully to the priest and follow what he chants."

They had set up a small fire. The priest had started his chants and indicated with his head where he wanted me to sit. It was too hot and all at once I did not want to do this.

"Come on Damu...come on...it will be over soon. Don't you want *Thaatha'*[5]s soul to have safe passage?"

I did not know what that meant, nor did I care. I shook myself free and ran upstairs to the terrace.

I let the cool breeze caress my face. All around me I saw rooftops, with washing lines extending to miles. Clothes billowed in the afternoon wind. Footsteps followed me upstairs. It was Rekha again.

"Damu, I am sorry. I know you are sad. I am sad too. But this is something that needs to be done."

"Why can't Bala or Malathi do it? Or you?"

"Because *Thaatha* wanted it to be you. Besides, you know women cannot perform last rites."

I did not know this.

The fire was hot and the priest kept glaring at me. I sat submissively, throwing in the oil, mouthing the prayers, staring at the old man who would never speak again, nor teach me how to play chess.

THREE MONTHS AGO

The old man was having a meeting in his room. Malathi kept hovering at the door. I thought she had done more than enough dusting when she suddenly looked at me.

"Damu, why don't you go and sit inside with *Thaatha*? I am sure he wouldn't mind."

I shook my head. I was enjoying my book and didn't want to leave my spot.

"Oh, but it is so hot there, Damu! You'll be so much cooler under the fan. I will make you some *mysore pak* if you listen."

I loved *mysore pak*[6], the ghee filled sugary dessert that melted in my mouth and would have walked to Siberia for some. I peeled myself off the swing in the courtyard and opened *Thaatha's* door.

"What is it?" He growled at me over his half-moon specs. He was surrounded by papers and a slight, officious looking man was pointing something out to him.

I was surprised. The old man never growled, not at me at any rate.

"I am hot." I declared and promptly planted myself in his armchair, near the fan.

He looked at me somewhat suspiciously, then asked me to shut the door.

"Krishnan, I will have to appoint a guardian. He is too young to..."

"Yes, Mr Subramanium, he is too young. However, that is not the only problem. Even at twenty one, will he be capable enough...?"

Thaatha cleared his throat quite dramatically.

"So, what do you suggest?"

"A life guardian, with a stipend perhaps. Enough to keep him or her in comfort, but not enough to make a huge dent in the capital."

"How does one ensure that the boy will be taken care of?"

"My firm will do monthly checks on his wellbeing, for a small fee, of course."

"Of course. But make it fortnightly."

There was more shuffling of papers and lengthy talk of sums that I half followed. My book got more interesting and soon I was swallowed up whole by the adventures of the intrepid seven.

Malathi plied me with *mysore pak* and asked me lots of questions.

"Was *Thaatha* very busy?"

"Mmmm-hmmm."

"Did he talk of a will?"

"No."

"Was Mr Krishnan saying anything to *Thaatha* about the house?"

I tired of this silly game and had quite enough *mysore pak* for a while. So, to shut her up, I said, "They were talking about appointing someone as my guardian and giving them money to take care of me."

Then I went back to my book, but not before catching her startled look.

THE CREMATORIUM HAD FILLED with people as well. The old man had been popular. I knew he had been respected from the way someone or the other would come and consult with him every day. Here, however, there were people sobbing, and talking about what a great man he had been.

Rekha led me to a quiet corner.

"Damu, you do understand what you have to do now?"

I did not understand any of it, so I just stared blankly at her.

"You will have to light the pyre."

"What's that?"

"That is the wooden structure that *Thaatha* will be placed upon, before you set it alight."

"But then he will burn."

"Yes, Damu, but that is only his body. His soul is already making its journey."

"I don't want to burn *Thaatha*."

Bala came over. He looked tired and slightly pale. Rekha and he exchanged a look.

Then he said, "Perhaps I should do it. It is too much for the boy."

"Those were not his wishes."

"I am tired of listening to 'these were his wishes', 'those were not his wishes'. What about us? Are we not family? Everything... everything has been about the boy. I am tired of it!"

Rekha reached forward and touched him on the arm

"I am sorry Bala. I know it has been very hard for you."

Malathi appeared at his elbow and hissed at Rekha, "You leave my husband alone!"

"But *Akka*, I was just..."

"Don't you dare call me your sister! I know all your wily ways. You tried ensnaring him the last time as well. If I hadn't found out in time, I would have been without a husband or a home. You keep your filthy hands off him!"

Rekha looked abashed and steered me away from them.

"Damu, please. Do this for me, and I will not bother you again. I am only here for you and for *Thaatha*. Once this is over, I will not darken your doorstep anytime soon."

I nodded and soon found myself near the pyre. *Thaatha* had been laid out on the platform. His body was covered with kindling, but I could still see his face, which had been left uncovered. Someone handed me a flare. I walked around the pyre five times, then touched it to the kindling. It ignited immediately. I stepped back and watched *Thaatha* go up in flames. Crematorium workers prodded at his body to make sure the fire spread evenly. At one point, there was a loud bang.

"Oh, that's just the skull exploding..." someone said.

We stood there for a while watching the fire blaze long and high, and then were told we could leave.

"I will come back and collect the ashes tomorrow." Bala said to one of the men there.

Most people had left now. We slowly made our way to the waiting taxi. Rekha hugged me hard and wiped a tear off her face.

"Ahhh, Damu. I don't know when I will see you next. Promise you will come and visit me?"

I nodded again. I felt exhausted from the day's events and just wanted to lie down.

FIVE YEARS AGO

Rekha held my hand and walked into the large house. I had never seen such high ceilings before. My house had been small and had consisted of just two rooms. This house seemed to have many many rooms.

"Is that him?" The man looked at me from his rocking chair.

"Yes." Rekha answered softly.

"Why did it take you so long?"

"I was trying to manage on my own. I didn't know if you would entertain any communication from us."

"Hmmm. How long has it been?"

"Six months."

"Car accident, you say?"

"Yes. They were on their way to Tirupathi to offer prayers."

"Was the boy with them?"

"Yes."

"And has he said anything?"

"No... but... you have to understand... he does not speak much anyway."

The man looked at me again. He called me over to him. I refused to budge.

"He has my temperament... and my eyes..."

We were allocated a room. I slept with Rekha. She held me and soothed me through my nightly terrors.

"Shhhh, Damu, shhhh. You are safe now."

I was introduced to Bala and Malathi. They tried their best to disguise their shock and dismay, but even at seven years of age, I could sense I was not wanted.

"What does this mean, *Appa*[7]? Why have you taken him in? Give that girl some money and be rid of them."

"Why are you threatened by the boy, Bala?"

"Threatened? What nonsense! I just feel that after all these years, and all the hurt caused, it makes no sense to bring him into our lives. We know nothing about them. She is a low caste, just like her brother. And he... he is a strange little creature. Do you not find it odd how he says nothing, just stares at us all the time?"

"Be that as it may, this is my opportunity to make amends for all my wrongs. I will provide for the boy as long as I am alive. He is here to stay Bala, and your wife and you had better get used to the idea."

"And what will you tell him as he grows up? Will you tell him about how you threw his mother out when you found out she was pregnant with that low-caste's child? Or how, when she begged for forgiveness, you refused to listen to her pleas? How will you explain the fact that you never wished to see your grandson's face till he appeared before you after his parents' death?"

"Enough! I have revisited my sins any number of times. You do not have to remind me of anything."

I DREAMT OF THEM OFTEN. Her, with her slanted green eyes and lustrous brown hair that she would knot at the nape of her neck. The smell of the jasmine flowers she would wear around the knot. The big red dot of *kumkumam* she would align between her eyebrows. He, with his charcoal black skin, his great big hugs and a laugh that would boom and reverberate in our little home.

Then I would dream of them dead. Their bodies a mangled mess of skin and bones and blood. I would wake up drenched in sweat, shaking in terror, unable to voice my utter, utter desolation.

I STAYED in my room for three days after the old man's death. Bala and Malathi tried to persuade me to join them for meals. I refused to answer. They took to leaving a plate of food outside the door. They would often find it untouched. Some of the time though, overcome with hunger, I would demolish the contents.

I could tell they were worried. They did not want to be saddled with a twelve-year-old boy who was not right in the head.

On the fourth day, the lawyer came home.

The conference was to be held in the large living room. Chairs had been placed in a semi-circle around *Thaatha*'s rocking chair. The lawyer looked discomfited to be placed in what had hitherto been *Thaatha*'s symbol of authority and assurance. He kept trying to control the chair's movement with his feet planted securely on the floor. Every so often though, he would forget, and the chair would jerk involuntarily, startling him no end.

"It is my sad duty to inform you of the contents of Mr. Subramani-um's will. However, I cannot begin, till all the family members are present."

Bala looked around the room.

"Mr. Krishnan, we are all here. As you know, our family has shrunk over the years. My father broke his ties with a lot of our relatives. Besides, we have no children of our own. So, I cannot imagine who else you are expecting?"

When Rekha walked in, Malathi jumped to her feet.

"I knew it! Didn't I say, Bala, didn't I? He has left her and the wretched boy everything. We will be out on the streets. That conniving old..."

"Mrs. Subramanium, please calm down. I haven't read out the will yet."

Malathi sat down in a huff, shooting venomous looks our way.

He started reading out the legal document in a low, monotonous voice. I rapidly tuned out, finding the proceedings dull to an extreme. My eyes wandered around the room. They took in the paintings *Thaatha* had on the walls, (expensive ones I knew, for Malathi had scolded me for trying to draw a moustache on the woman), the artefacts that decorated the shelves, the silk curtains that hung over the windows. Occasionally, I caught a gasp or a mutter. My name was mentioned several times. Rekha squeezed my hand now and again. It's only when she tried shaking me awake, that I realised I must have fallen asleep.

The lawyer was gathering up his papers and saying, "I will, of course, confirm it all in writing. However, if everyone is in agreement, then the arrangement can begin straight away."

When he had left, Malathi sat with her head in her hands.

"To think... to think... he would do this to his own son!"

"Hush, dear, hush. The boy is awake. Anyway, it's not like we've been left penniless. As long as we have him here, we can live in the house too."

"And what about her?"

"You will have to learn to get along with her, Malathi. And I swear, I will not... I never... you misunderstood..."

Rekha took me to my room.

"Damu, I will be living here... with you! Isn't that wonderful?

Thaatha knew how much you meant to me. Come here! Give me a hug."

FOUR YEARS AGO

The thunder had woken him up. His heart was pounding. His hands searched for Rekha, but found an empty spot, still warm. Panic stricken, he stumbled out of bed, looking for her.

They were locked in an embrace in a cool corner of the kitchen. Bala kept running his hands down her back, pulling her closer, nipping at her ear, as she giggled softly.

He turned around as quietly as he had come in. His eyes met with another pair of green eyes. The old man shook his head lightly, put a finger to his lips and then ushered him out gently.

SIXTY TWO YEARS LATER

I live alone now, in this house of secrets and lies. Malathi was the first one to die. They called it cancer. I knew it was a broken heart. It didn't take Bala and Rekha long after to tie the knot. They had children together. Children that had been provided for, in the will. What foresight father had, Bala had exclaimed.

I was well looked after. There was always enough food, enough clothes, enough education. As for love, is there ever enough?

When I was thirty, they moved away. Each of them living their own lives, in their own ways.

I am an old man now, just like *Thaatha* was, when he died. I sit in his rocking chair, and watch the world pass me by. I think of him, of his genuine desire to right his wrongs. And then, I think of that strange line in his will:

I want all of Damu's family to live together and take care of him, and one another. I want this to be a happy family again.

Of course, he knew then, as well as I know now; there are no happy endings.

6

THE CONSEQUENCE OF
CONTRADICTION

S HE wrapped the sari carefully around her, making sure that the pleats fell together in tandem, not one shorter or longer than the other. The *pallu*[1] was the last fold of the sari, and with a graceful swish, it was over her left shoulder, falling at exactly the point she needed, just below her knee. With a self-satisfied pirouette, she flicked her hair back and examined her face. Still no lines. She was lucky to have been blessed with her mother's beautiful Asian complexion, and at forty-five, prided herself on looking at least ten years younger.

"Diksha...how much longer?" called out Ajay. Twenty four years, and he still didn't understand the pleasure that she took in the ceremony of dressing up. *Shringar*[2], they had called it in India. She remembered being part of a dance ballet that explored the concept of *Shringar*. The preparation, the anticipation, the actual act of beautifying the self. The grace and the comeliness.

"Ten minutes!" She called back, sensing his irritation, and perversely enjoying it.

. . .

IT WAS AN ANNIVERSARY PARTY. Everyone was dressed to the nines. They still turned to look when she walked in. She enjoyed being the cynosure of all eyes. Always had.

"Turquoise blue? I thought you said you were wearing green?" Rima questioned her sourly.

"I changed my mind."

"Well, it does look good on you. Sushma won't be pleased."

The hostess was wearing turquoise blue too, but despite her best efforts looked like a dowdy partridge masquerading as a peacock.

"Sushma, how lovely you look!" Diksha air kissed her, ensuring the photographer got her best angle. "Where is Vinod?"

"Oh, he's sorting out last minute stuff. Your children didn't come?"

"No, Aria has her exams prep... And Akash... well, you know boys..."

With a shrug, she moved away to say hello to the other wives. They were all polite. They always were. But they hated her. She had refused to grow old and frumpy like them. She enjoyed her liquor and the company of men, and she had a husband who allowed her all these freedoms without censure.

She had always assumed that living in the US would mean taking these liberties for granted. Yet discovered to her dismay that the Indian community in Chicago was even more narrow minded, orthodox and conservative than the one she'd left behind in Delhi. In that stultifying environment, she'd had the choice of toeing the line or rebelling. She'd chosen the latter.

"There you are!" He pinched her bottom discreetly.

"Vinod, stop it! It's your anniversary party."

"It's also another anniversary." He winked at her. She suppressed her grin and thrust her glass at him. "Get me another whiskey and go mingle. I don't want to set tongues wagging."

The evening passed, as it always did, in a haze of whiskey and tall tales. She stayed in the men's corner, provocatively dropping her *pallu* now and again to let them glimpse her cleavage. It never failed to amuse her.

· · ·

LATER THAT NIGHT, as she unwrapped the sari, she caught Ajay's eyes in the mirror.

"You looked hot tonight."

She stopped and waited.

"They wanted you so badly. I could see it in their eyes."

She held her breath.

"You're a whore! A fucking whore."

With that, he turned his back on her and let out a little fart, before falling asleep almost immediately.

"THIS IS THE BEAN, *Mamu*[3]. A very famous sculpture by Anish Kapoor."

"Too hot beta. Too hot. I need to sit down."

Exasperated, she sat down once again. At this rate they'd never get to see anything. She examined her uncle and aunt with fresh eyes. They really weren't that old. Mid-sixties wasn't old, was it? Yet, there they were, in their traditional attire, incongruously paired with sneakers and baseball caps, insisting on ten-minute breaks every half hour. Why spend lakhs of Rupees, travel thousands of miles, and then want to sit indoors in air conditioning watching Indian television? It baffled her.

She loved Chicago. Her adopted city that had embraced her, taken her to its high rise bosom and laid her gently by the shores of its lake. She loved the extremes of its blistering Summers and its freezing Winters. Spring brought her hope, and Fall, a beautiful melancholy. She couldn't imagine going back to the noise and pollution of India. She had little to return to as it was. *Mamu* and *Mami*[4] were her only living relatives, and she wanted to show off her city to them. Preen in its beauty and bask in the worldliness it had bestowed upon her. They were not making it easy.

"Can we have *daal roti*[5] tonight beta?" *Mami* looked at her hopefully. "That sushi has given me constipation."

. . .

THE BUTTER CHICKEN had turned out well. Even if she thought so herself. It had been a while since she'd cooked Indian food. Yet memories of her mother's instructions had risen to the surface like it was yesterday that she had been taught the nuances of *masalas* [6]and *tarkas*[7].

Aria swung her legs back and forth, perched on the kitchen counter top.

"Who is coming to dinner again Mom?"

"Some friend of *Mamu's*. No - actually, his friend's son. He's working in Chicago, and you know how these old bonds operate. His father must've said he needs to visit..."

"That's why you're cooking up a storm? Why not just order some pizza?"

"You know they don't care for western food."

"And I don't care for all this smelly Indian food!"

"Aria! Have some respect. They are like your grandparents..."

With a lazy shrug, Aria slid off. "Happy cooking Mom. I'll be out tonight."

"What! Again...?"

Aria had already left the kitchen. With a sigh, Diksha returned to peeling the cucumber. How obedient she had been as a young girl. Her family had wanted her to go to a college near home. She had agreed. No riding in buses to the North Campus. No exciting freshers parties. No boyfriends. No late night soirees. God! She'd had a boring youth. No wonder she was making up for it now.

Her thoughts circled back to Vinod. It was getting awkward now. He was getting sloppy, and the initial thrill had long since evaporated. She had to find a way to break it off before the proverbial hit the fan.

THAT EVENING she decided to dress casually. After all, she had to do all the running around. Despite *Mami's* protestations, she wanted her to relax and enjoy the evening. She did enough in India. This was her vacation too, and she didn't want her spending it in the kitchen making *chapatis*[8] for their guest.

So it was a slightly sweaty and harried Diksha that answered the door to Rahul. Her eyes widened slightly at the sight of the good looking young man on her doorstep. She noted his response. A quick, surprised appraisal before bland politeness took its place.

She tried not to flirt. After all he was nearly twenty years younger. But her nature could not be denied. As the evening progressed, and the wine worked to loosen inhibitions, he leaned over to her.

"That was the best butter chicken I've eaten in years. Tell me the name of the restaurant, and I'll promise you anything in return."

In mock horror, she leaned back. "How dare you imply I had this delivered! I've been slaving over the stove all day..."

He laughed then and stretched out his long legs. "Then I suppose I'll have to promise myself to you, in return for the recipe."

She sensed *Mami's* discomfiture and avoided her eye. It was only harmless banter. Their generation was simply not used to it.

HE TRAILED kisses down her back, stopping at just above the slope of her curvy *derriere*.

"You are incredibly sexy," he whispered.

She laughed and turned to face him. "Not too old then?"

"Like wine. Like a rare Bordeaux - full bodied, silky and luscious."

"And you are wasting time...Come on, we don't have long..."

VINOD HAD BEEN a pain to shake off. It had taken several weeks of avoiding his calls and ignoring him at social gatherings for the message to finally penetrate. He still threw her perplexed and slightly hurt looks whenever they came across one another. She studiously ignored him, focussing instead on the heady feeling of being desired and pursued.

Rahul had not been subtle. With all the gusto of youth, he had made his ardour evident. From the thank you flowers to the cards that followed to the phone calls inviting her to coffee, he left no stone unturned in his pursuit of her. She found it exciting and unnerving.

That she would succumb was more a matter of when rather than why.

His apartment had the feel of a bachelor pad - largely unused, and mostly neglected. He had wasted no time on preliminaries, and taken her on the couch, in the first of many lustful adventures. He was a masterful lover, making her body quiver to his command. The afterglow of their lovemaking would encase her in a golden hue, till their next rendezvous, and the next and the next.

She didn't want to examine her feelings too closely. She had been in other extramarital relationships. There was an understanding between her and Ajay. She didn't question his activities, and he turned a blind eye to hers. This tacit accord had worked over the years. The children knew nothing, and to their friends, they were an ideal couple. Yet this time, she felt something in her changing. Rahul was the man she wished Ajay could be. Erudite and accomplished, with a strong sense of purpose and a determination to succeed. Ajay, for all his money and business acumen, would never be as sophisticated as the young man who wooed her with such urgency.

"YOU'LL never believe this…" Rahul blew smoke rings towards the ceiling, as she lay dozing next to him. "Your uncle has been in touch with my dad…"

"And?" She responded sleepily.

"They want me to meet your daughter."

"What?!" She sat up, startled.

"Your uncle seems to think we'd make a good match."

"But…but… Aria is only twenty! She's far too young…"

He looked at her and laughed. "I think that may be the least of your worries."

ALL evening she agonised about what her uncle was conspiring to do. Ajay had just returned from Denver, and she brought it up with him.

"Yes, *Mamu* had sent me an email about it, and I said why not?"

"Why not? Ajay! Aria is so young. She hasn't even completed her education."

"She's not the most academic of children anyway, and in our family, we marry the girls off young. You were not much older when I married you."

"She will never agree. She's far too independent. Besides, what do we know about this Rahul anyway, huh?" Superstitiously she crossed her fingers behind her back.

"Well, his parents are visiting in June. I've asked your uncle to arrange a meeting. We can get to know the family and introduce the children. I've heard he's doing well. A hotshot lawyer in some big firm. Didn't you say he was a nice chap too?"

Silently, she digested the news. June was two weeks away. This could be a complete disaster! Or maybe not. An idea took shape in her mind.

"YOU HAVE TO SAY NO!" She insisted, batting his hands away. She'd been trying to talk sense to him but he was intent on unbuttoning her top.

"Why?" He finally leaned back with a sardonic grin.

"Because...because..." She spluttered, "She's only a child... and you and I..."

"Yes?" He resumed removing her blouse. "You and I what?"

"We're lovers!" She spat out angrily, moving out of his reach. "It would be wrong...incestuous..."

"*Les Liaisons Dangeureuses...*" He commented with a wicked glint in his eyes.

"Be polite but firm. Say she's too young. Say you want to concentrate on your career. It'll blow over soon enough."

"Alright. Alright. Now come on over here."

. . .

WITH A STRANGE SENSE OF FOREBODING, Diksha wore the most conservative of her salwar suits that evening. Aria had been oddly compliant in agreeing to meet Rahul. She had even deigned to dress in a somewhat sober fashion. Diksha couldn't help but feel a sense of pride when she looked at her beautiful daughter. Aria had the same willowy loveliness that she had once possessed. But underneath it all was a fiery temperament, and an implacable will.

"Are you sure you're okay with all this darling? You know there is no pressure. You *can* say no. You know that, right?"

"Oh mom! You worry too much." Aria planted a swift kiss on her cheek and headed out.

ON A SCALE of 1 to 10, it was an 11 in terms of disaster. Ajay and Rahul's parents had gotten along like a house on fire, talking common friends, common schools and all the commonality that came from belonging to the same town many moons ago. Worse, however, was the look that she'd spotted in Rahul's eyes when Aria walked in. An astonishment, and an awe in the face of her beauty. She'd suddenly felt very old and had to retreat to the kitchen to compose herself.

When the last of the brandies had been consumed, and the last cigars smoked, it was lightly suggested that the young folk might want to get better acquainted. Aria had blushed, and Rahul had agreed eagerly. Diksha felt sick, and pleading a headache left Ajay to conclude the evening.

"RAHUL, please pick up! You've been ignoring my calls long enough. Please!"

Once again, it went into voicemail.

All her pleadings with Aria had fallen on deaf ears. Aside of being smitten with her dashing young suitor, Aria saw this as an escape from the tedium of studies and jobs, and an entree into an exciting life of parties, travel and unencumbered sex. They were already discussing venues and dates. Diksha felt desperate and alone in her misery.

In a last-ditch attempt, she waited in his stairwell, cornering him just as he was entering his apartment.

"Rahul!"

He flinched when he saw her, and then covered his reaction with a polite mask.

"Diksha, how nice to see you here. How are you? Long time, hey?"

"Don't fob me off with this crap!" She spat.

He ushered her in quickly, the mask dropping just as fast.

"What the hell do you want?"

"You know what I want. I want you to leave Aria alone."

"No can do."

"You don't love her."

"You don't know that."

"What sick game are you playing Rahul?"

He leaned back against the wall. "Tell me something Diksha. Would you leave your husband for me?"

"What? No! And you wouldn't want that either. It was always a no strings attached thing."

"Well then, how can you begrudge me the next best thing?"

"Rahul, I'm not sure what your agenda is, but please, I beg you... this is my child. She is only an innocent."

"Not from the way she performs dearest Mom-in-law to be. She could teach you a few tricks."

Her palm connected with his face with such force that she nearly dislocated her arm. She ran out, her face flaming, her heart beating an uneven tattoo.

What do I do? What do I do?

DELHI was just as hot and polluted as she remembered. Aria wouldn't stop coughing, making her point loudly. She'd refused to exchange a word with her on the flight. Not even the promise of a magnificent trousseau could puncture the grand sulk.

As she lay next to *Mami*, enjoying her afternoon siesta, the knot in her chest loosened somewhat. From the first moment that she had walked into the bougainvillea covered bungalow, she had felt a sense of peace. *Mamu*, *Mami*, Home. Memories of her childhood had come rushing back. The childless couple that had taken her orphan self in and given her love and opportunity and a future. How had it become so messed up? Why?

The Blind school she took Aria to on the pretext of buying candles, was only an excuse. Years ago, *Mamu* had taken her there. In her selfish, teenage years she had often wallowed in self-pity at being orphaned so young. He had made her sit in on classes, help with serving the food, and in his own exquisitely insightful manner, opened her eyes to her good fortune.

She watched Aria respond to the children around her in the same fashion. She was reticent at first, and then gradually she volunteered herself, playing, laughing, clapping and singing with the happy souls that surrounded her. Diksha saw no handicap in anyone there, but herself.

"When were you going to tell her, *beta*[9]?" *Mami* enquired gently, "About Rahul and yourself?"

Diksha felt her mouth go slack. She had forgotten that this little old lady had all the powers of incision that a mother possessed.

"How can I, *Mami*? What will she think of me? She will never ever respect me again."

"Diksha, is respect more important to you than honesty? This is your daughter's future. You cannot let her make her decision without knowing all the facts."

"Why did you let this go ahead *Mami*?" Diksha questioned bitterly.

"I tried to dissuade your uncle, but he was adamant. He saw us forging a stronger bond with the Sharmas. He did not suspect what I suspected. Besides *beta*, isn't it time you examined your own actions? Every action has a consequence. Isn't it time you owned up to your responsibility?"

· · ·

THAT NIGHT as the fan swung in lazy arcs above them, Diksha tossed and turned, her mind in tumult. Everything hung in balance here. Her child's happiness, her own marriage, her reputation, the future of her relationship with her family.

It was true that every action had a consequence. Her contradictory behaviour, her unhappy marriage, her wilfulness, her selfishness had long been leading to this day of reckoning. Yet, it was a consequence she could not shy away from any longer.

Impulsively she shook Aria awake. Groggy and irritated, she sat up.

"What is it Mom?"

"Aria, I have something to tell you."

7

LOVE JIHAD

London 2017

Arti looked at Mohsin and sighed. "How long can we carry on like this? I'm getting tired of all this secrecy."

He squeezed her hand briefly before replacing it on the steering wheel and turning his attention to the road again. "Not long. I've nearly convinced *Ammi* [1] and *Abbu* [2] to meet you. It's your turn now."

"Mohsin, Mum and Dad will never agree! You know they can be quite conservative..."

"Arti, it's the 21st century. It's not like I'm going to put you in a hijab and keep you under lock and key. We are liberal Muslims. If it weren't for the fact that my parents had their hearts set on Nusrat, their friend's daughter as my prospective wife, they'd barely notice you're a different religion."

He parked the car in front of Premier Inn and turned to look at her.

"We aren't children anymore. We have the right to make our own decisions. If we love one another and choose to marry, then really it's no one's business."

"Mohsin, I'm their only child, I can't disappoint them. I just have to work on convincing them. Give me a few more months to soften them up. I'm sure they'll agree once they've met you, and you've worked your charm on them, hey?"

"Charm, huh?" he nuzzled her. "Let me charm you some more princess. Ready to go inside?"

Later, as they lay together in the tangled sheets, Arti propped herself up on her forearms to look at a dozing Mohsin. She couldn't imagine what he'd seen in her. Two years ago, when he'd walked into their office as a new recruit, he'd sent all the women into a tizzy. Even the married ones. He could have had his pick. There was the leggy Zoe, or the voluptuous Marie, or even the petite Hiromi. Yet, he'd chosen her.

When she'd first asked him why, he'd laughed and changed the topic. As they'd grown more serious about one another, he'd explained. "I'm tired of meaningless flings Arti. These girls just want to have a bit of fun and move on. I want something long term, something stable. As an Asian girl, I'm sure you understand?"

She did understand. Her parents had been married thirty years. Theirs had been an arranged match. They'd met just once to approve each other, and everything else had been sorted by their families. For them, just as for her, marriage was for life.

As a second generation Indian and the daughter of immigrant parents, she had been given all kinds of freedom. From the way she dressed, to the higher education she pursued, to her career in the City, her parents had never once objected to anything. An unspoken understanding underlined these liberties though. An understanding that when it came to marriage, she would take the same route as them. She would settle for a husband they picked; a well-educated, well settled Hindu boy from their own community.

How would they react to Mohsin?

Jaipur 2017

Bela hurried towards the dispensary, her mother's admonishments ringing in her ears. The narrow, bustling streets of her locality were teeming with all kinds of traffic. Cars, people and animals jostled for space and as she stopped to let a cyclist through, an arm snaked out and grabbed her. Her startled scream was cut short by a hand placed quickly on her mouth. As she looked up at the familiar face, her body relaxed.

"Yusuf!"

"I've missed you! Where have you been Bela?"

"Baba has been ill, and Maa hasn't been able to cope, what with Amar disappearing on us again. So, I took a few days off college. But, why are you here?" She looked around furtively. "What if someone sees us?"

"I don't care! It's been torture not being able to talk to you. Look at what I've got you..."

Bela, distracted and worried about being spotted with Yusuf, barely glanced at his outstretched hand. She looked at the people milling around her and decided the best course would be to duck into the nearest *chai* stall. With a tilt of her head, she signalled her intention. Following her cue, they stepped into the makeshift shelter and ordered a *chai* [3]each. Blowing into the earthen cup, she briefly allowed herself to inhale the spicy mix of cardamom and cinnamon, settling her jangled nerves.

"Look!" Yusuf held out his hand again. A shiny cellphone sat in the palm of his hand.

"I can't accept this." Bella looked at him sadly. She knew he could ill afford to buy her such extravagant presents, but she could not take any chances. In their two room flat, a cellphone would be easily spotted.

"Hide it," he urged, reading her mind. "Turn off the ringer. Only use it to SMS me. Bela please, I need to know that you are okay."

Reluctantly she slipped it into her bag.

"I've put a pre-paid sim card in it. Just Rs,100 but it should last you a while. When it runs out, let me know and I'll top it up."

"I have to go now Yusuf. Maa told me to hurry with Baba's medicines. I'll see you in a few days, okay?"

"Message me everyday... Promise?"

"Yes, yes."

She hurried out, glancing around her, on the lookout for any familiar faces. Then she turned once and mouthed 'I love you' to his desolate figure, holding two cups of unconsumed *chai*.

London 2017

"How long have you been dating him, Arti?" Shabnam asked as she glanced at the menu. The bar was buzzing with Friday evening revellers. Ties had been loosened and the heels had come out to play.

"Eight months." Arti looked at Shabnam's long, hot pink nails and wondered how she ever got any work done with them.

"Is that long enough? I mean, I know he's your first and all that, but come on... Asian dudes can be real chauvinists. Why do you think I'm with Mark?"

"Mohsin is not like that at all. He comes from a real liberal background and doesn't expect me to convert or anything. Shabz, at least meet him no? I think you'll like him."

It had been hard enough confessing her secret to anyone, let alone be met by this kind of resistance. She had thought Shabnam would understand, particularly as she had bucked the traditional route herself.

"I don't think my liking him will make any difference honey! It's your peeps that have to agree. All I'm saying is, give it a bit more time. Get to know him some more. Maybe live in, like Mark and I?"

"Look where that got you! Your family won't even speak with you."

"Yeah well, at least they're not shipping me off to Pakistan to marry my third cousin! Sod that. I'm living my life on my own terms."

"That's all I want as well. To marry the man I love. What religion he was born into, or which country his parents came from shouldn't affect our future. We are British now. Born and raised in this country."

"Hmmmm." Shabnam pulled out a cigarette from her purse. "Look, from my experience of Muslim men - my dad included - they like their women to toe the line. I know you aren't a major rebel or anything, but are you ready to let him dictate terms to you?"

"Shabz!! For the love of God - Mohsin isn't like that!" Her eyes welled up. This was tougher than she'd expected.

"Hey, hey honey, why the tears? I'm just teasing. I'm sure he's a lovely guy. Oh, come on...look, our wine is here. Cheer up, will you?"

Jaipur 2017

Bela wrapped the towel around her head like a turban before stepping out of the bathroom. She had tried to use just a third of a bucket to wash her hair. The municipality only gave a half hour window for water collection at 5am in the mornings, so they had to be careful not to run out before then.

Her mother was sitting on the verandah chopping vegetables for lunch. Bela joined her on the *charpoy*,[4] taking the towel off her head, and letting her hair dry in the morning sunshine.

"Maa?"

"Hmmmm?"

"Where is Amar, do you think?"

She sensed her mother stiffen, even as she lay supine next to her, her long hair spilling over the edge of the *charpoy*.

"That good-for-nothing son of mine must be wandering the streets like a stray dog shouting '*Har Har Mahadev*'![5]" She sniffed. "I wish your Baba had never taken him to that conman. We wouldn't have lost our son this way."

"Guru *ji* is running for elections this time."

"So I see. Why a Guru needs to join politics is beyond me! As I said all along, he is a conman and a fraudster. He's brainwashed the youth of this city, and now they lap up every word of his like it's *somras* [6]from the Gods."

"Maa - why is Guru *ji* so anti Muslim? They are human beings just like us. Look at Shabana or Fauzia or even Mir *bhai jaan*[7]. They are all so nice."

"Bela, you don't understand politics. Of course, they are nice people. I don't have a problem with them. But a politician needs an angle. This charlatan Guru's angle is that *Mussalmans*[8] are evil and they are trying to spread their religion through violence or having too many babies or marrying our Hindu girls. Look at all his followers, including your imbecile brother. People will believe anything if you frighten them enough."

"Anju... Anju..." Baba's voice, weakened from illness, called out to his wife. Maa hastily set the vegetable dish down to hurry inside. Bela sighed and sat up to finish chopping the rest. The topic of Yusuf would have to wait for another opportune moment.

London 2017

"Arti, wear a sari for the wedding this time."

"Why mum? I prefer the salwar suit, and I have that pretty blue one I could wear tonight."

"I wish you would just listen once in a while without arguing back."

"I'm not arguing, I'm just putting forward my point of view." She stuck her tongue out as her mother mock rapped her on the knuckles. "Anyway, why all this sari business? It's just Seema auntie's daughter's wedding. Not like a close relative or anything..."

"Well, I guess I'll just have to tell you then." Her mother sat down on the bed and looked at her solemnly. "There's a boy we want to introduce you to. He's come from America. He's a doctor there, and Seema thinks he might be a good match for you."

Arti tried to keep a straight face but her heart was hammering so hard against her rib cage she wondered if her mother could hear it.

"I'm not ready for marriage mum! I'm only twenty five. There's so much more I want to do. I want to travel the world, progress in my career...so much more... This isn't a good time!"

"Darling, there's no such thing as a good or a bad time. We're not asking you to marry him tomorrow. Just meet him. His background is sound, and these are just the preliminaries anyway. We still have to meet the family and all that. Come on now, get your blouse and petticoat sorted. I'm going to let you borrow my green sari."

Her mum kissed her on the forehead and left to fetch the sari. Arti sat dumbstruck, her thoughts crashing into each other. She had always known this day would come but hadn't expected it quite this soon. Could she even broach the subject of Mohsin when he hadn't yet asked her to marry him? What if her parents really liked this doctor fellow? Would they force her hand? What would Mohsin think? Maybe it was a good thing? Maybe this would worry him enough to take the next step?

Mum walked in with the sari draped on one arm. "Why are you still sitting there? Get up! We have to leave in an hour..."

As it was, it wasn't the most torturous evening ever. Amit turned out to be a nice guy. He spoke to her respectfully and actually listened to her responses. Besides he was really quite attractive in an Americanised, laid back way. There was a slight awkwardness between them that soon dissipated. If she hadn't been so head over heels mad about Mohsin, Amit would have been difficult to dismiss.

In the car, Dad said, "I liked him Arti. What did you think?"

She shrugged, and keeping her voice as neutral as possible, said, "He was alright."

<u>Jaipur 2017</u>

Bela left early for her tuition classes. As far as Maa knew they started at 4:30pm when in actual fact they started a half hour later. But it gave her just a little bit of time with Yusuf; just enough to spin dreams of a future together that looked increasingly impossible.

They sat together on the park bench, discreetly holding hands and letting go as soon as any passer by walked past. The moral police in the city didn't need much excuse, and they tried to stay as inconspicuous as possible.

"We just have another three months of college. What then Bela?"

"Then we look for jobs close to each other and keep on meeting this way."

"You can't be serious! Jobs aren't easy to find, and what if I don't get one in this city? What if I have to go to Delhi or Mumbai? What then?"

"Then we put up with the separation till the time is right."

Yusuf looked at her wonderingly. "Do you even love me? How can you be so matter of fact about everything?"

Bela sighed and looked down at her lap. She spoke softly. "Don't ever doubt my love Yusuf. But don't be foolish enough to think that this road we've set upon is an easy one. Look around you at what's happening in the country. Anti-muslim fervour has the nation in its grip. There are conspiracy theories fuelled by rumours and jingoism. My own brother is parading around mouthing slogans against the *Mussalmans*. How do you think our match will go down with my family or our community?"

"Then run away with me! Once we are married, they can't do a thing."

"Don't be silly. Run away where? Do what? You can't run away from yourself, and if I let my parents down this way, I'll never be able to forgive myself!"

Yusuf put his head in his hands. "I cannot see a way out."

"Patience, Yusuf, patience. It's the only way. We have our whole lives ahead of us. Let things calm down. My parents are not unreasonable people. Even Amar can be coaxed into seeing sense. It's only a matter of time. What's the rush anyway?"

They held hands a bit longer and then Bela stood up.

"I have to go. My student must be wondering where I am. I'll SMS you tonight, okay?"

Suddenly Yusuf reached out and embraced her to him violently.

"I can't wait anymore! I can't...I can't..."

Bela shook herself free, pushing at him with all her might. She ran as quickly as she could, his 'sorry' still ringing in her ears.

<u>London 2017</u>

"I'm pregnant!"

It came out in a rush, unplanned and slightly breathless. She had agonised on how and when to tell him. Planned elaborate speeches and scenarios. Ultimately, her outburst was neither timed nor tactful.

Mohsin looked shocked. As shocked as she'd felt when the two blue lines had appeared on the stick.

"Are you sure?"

"Yes." She nodded, reinforcing her certitude.

"That's wonderful news Arti!" he suddenly whooped, shocking everyone else in the coffee shop.

"Is it?" she wondered aloud.

What did this news even mean? She didn't feel particularly maternal. She had certainly not fallen pregnant to entrap Mohsin. She had thought marriage and babies lay somewhere in the future and would have been content to have her parents approve of their relationship first before any formal arrangements were made. Yet, this pregnancy had turned everything on its head.

"Of course, it is! Don't you see? Now, no one can disapprove our match. Not your parents nor mine. It's perfect." Mohsin grinned.

"Are you ready to be a father? I mean, don't you want to enjoy life a bit before then?"

"What can be more important or enjoyable than fatherhood, hey? Arti, stop stressing. This is the answer to all our problems."

Later that evening, as she sipped on her diet coke, Shabnam shook her head mournfully.

"What a mess you've created for yourself! What were you thinking? Any man who says that a baby is the answer to a problem needs his head examined. You've barely dated, and now this! I wish you'd come to me first."

"Before going to the father of the baby? Really Shabz!"

"Yes, really! Now that he knows there is no way for you to sort things out."

"Maybe I don't want to 'sort things out'? Maybe I'm quite content with how they are!"

"And that's why you're sitting here, looking like Hell and second guessing every move? Arti, get real! I've known you long enough to know that this isn't the way you would've wanted things to work out. Anyway, what's done is done. What's your next move?"

Jaipur 2017

"Amar is back," her mother whispered. "He's taking a nap. Be quiet and don't get into any arguments with him."

Bela nodded. She knew better than to try and reason with her brother. The easy camaraderie they had once shared had long since disappeared. When Baba had gone to the first of Guru *ji*'s meetings, he'd come back singing the praises of this unknown man who spoke so eloquently about the issues that plagued their country. He had dragged them all to the next meeting, and whilst Maa and she had seen through the facade almost immediately, Amar had been hypnotised by the saffron clad Guru and his sermon.

Before long he was one of the Guru's *chelas*[9]- a devotee, a follower. "An idiot!" Her mother had hissed to her non-plussed father.

At first, they seemed to do good: local community projects like planting more trees, organising water tankards for localities that suffered shortages, getting the Hindu temple to provide vaccinations for children, gratis. Their good deeds earned them enough fame to garner more followers, and as their numbers swelled, their agenda became clearer. The rhetoric turned acerbic and polarising. Muslims were to blame for everything. From terrorism to over population to lack of job opportunities to weak infrastructure and failing governments, Guru *ji* managed to pin it all on them. His followers spread the message far and wide, and the young and the easily swayed joined the band wagon.

The general populace was apathetic enough to dismiss the Guru as just another saffron clad clown looking for his fifteen minutes of fame. It was only when he decided to run for the elections that people woke up to the insidious danger he presented. By then it was too late. He had enough clout, enough money and enough adherents to win. He would have you believe that he had the entire pantheon of Hindu Gods behind him as well.

Amar lay sprawled on his stomach, deep snores emanating from him. Bela observed her brother silently. This was the same little boy who had followed her around lisping "*Didi*[10], *didi*...", hanging on to her every word, playing *pitthu* [11]and *oonch neech ka papda*.[12] When had he grown into this irascible, intolerant bigot of a man? Was there any getting through to him, or was he way past reason and rectitude?

London 2017

"*Ammi, Abba* - this is Arti." Mohsin presented her proudly to his parents. There was a moments silence and then Mohsin's mother came forward and embraced her warmly.

"So, you are the lovely girl we've been hearing about. Mohsin hasn't stopped talking about you for the whole of last week." She examined her once more. "Why he had to keep you a secret I do not know. Here we were planning for him to meet Nusrat, and there he was seeing you all along!"

Arti wasn't sure if she had imagined the sting in that innocuous statement and she looked towards Mohsin for reassurance.

"Oh, come on *Ammi*! Nusrat is like a little sister to me. I could no more imagine marrying her than I could Asma from back home."

He gave Arti's hand a quick squeeze.

"You work together?", his father asked.

"Yes, in the same office" Arti responded before adding, "but I'm planning to move to a different department soon."

"Why is that?"

"She's been given a promotion *Abba*," Mohsin interjected excitedly. "She's really good at what she does."

His father nodded and then exchanged a glance with his wife.

"Do you plan to keep working after...ahem...after...?"

Had Mohsin told them about the pregnancy? They had agreed to keep things quiet for the time being. Till they mutually decided whether or not they wished to proceed. How could he! Her parents knew nothing, and his parents were interrogating her on things she had not even processed fully herself. Mohsin caught her reproachful look and shrugged apologetically.

"I'm sorry Arti. I was so excited, it just slipped out."

His mother came over to her again and patted her on the head. "Don't worry *beti*,[13] we are not judging you or anything. It's not like we were never young. These things happen. We are just concerned that the stressful environment of the office may not be the right place for you at this time."

"Oh, I love my work and I don't find it stressful at all!"

"What about the marriage preparations? You will have to take some time out for those. And that reminds me! When do we get to meet your parents?"

Arti clasped her trembling hands together and whispered, "Soon."

Jaipur 2017

"What is this?" He questioned her, holding the cell phone in his hand.

"A phone" she responded softly, her insides quavering.

"Am I a *chut*[14]? Huh?? Do I look like a *chut* to you?" He grabbed her plait and yanked at it viciously.

"Amar!" Maa screamed, pulling him away. "What are you doing?"

"Ask this whore of a daughter that you have produced! Who is this 'Y' and why is he SMS-ing how much he loves her? How did she buy a phone when all you keep saying is that you have no money? Did she prostitute herself - this little bitch?!"

"How dare you talk to your sister like this! Get out...get out right now!"

"Anju!" Her father was leaning heavily on his stick. He held out his hand for the phone. The last SMS was clearly displayed on the screen. It must have come while she was cooking. Had she forgotten to turn the ringer off or had Amar been going through her stuff again? She thought she'd hidden the phone well enough. She should have known better.

"Where did you get this phone from?" Her father's voice was calm. Too calm.

"It was a gift - from a friend."

"A friend? Tell the truth, you little liar!" Amar screamed into her face, spraying her with his spittle. "Was it a lover or a customer? All the while pretending to be pure and good...! Giving tuitions, or whoring around, hey? *Kutti*[15]!"

Bela flinched, stepping back involuntarily. When had her soft, sensitive brother morphed into this rabid dog?

"Bela, who is this friend?"

She noticed how Baba said nothing to Amar but looked at her accusingly. Had it always been this way or was it just lately that she had picked up on it? Her only crime had been to be born a girl. In every other way she had tried to be the ideal child. Especially after Amar's defection to Guru *ji*. Her meagre earnings had supplemented the little income her father brought in, or they would have been unable to make ends meet. She worked hard at everything. She tried her best. Would it ever be good enough? No, she decided, it never would, or would any father let his daughter be subjected to such abuse?

She raised her chin defiantly and looked at him.

"His name is Yusuf, and he is my boyfriend. We intend to get married."

She never saw the blow coming, and just before her world went dark she heard her mother scream:

"Amar!!"

London 2017

Her father sat with his head in his hands. No words could have conveyed his utter disappointment in her better. Her mother was whispering into his ear, stroking his back as she did. Arti envied them their easy intimacy. She wondered if Mohsin and she would have an equally strong bond one day.

Which of her transgressions had unsettled them the most? The fact that she was pregnant or the fact that she was going to marry a Muslim man and not one of their choosing?

She had elected to do this alone. Mohsin had volunteered to be there, but as the only child of her parents, loved and indulged in every way, she felt she owed this to them. No smoke screens, just the plain, unvarnished truth.

She had expected anger, tears, recrimination, not this cold silence and withdrawal.

"Dad?"

He shook his head, unable to look at her.

"Arti, leave us for a bit," Mum said, "We need time to think things through."

She went to her bedroom and sat on the bed. The tears trickled down her cheeks silently. It had never been her intention to hurt her parents. She loved them too much for that. Yet, how could she have planned who she would fall in love with and when?

Her mother came in and sat on the bed with her. She took her hand in hers and patted it.

"I can't lie and say this hasn't been a shock, Arti. We wanted so much more for you; expected so much more of you. Yet, ultimately all that matters is your happiness. If, as you say, this boy makes you happy, and you intend to go ahead with this marriage and pregnancy, then you have our blessings."

"Oh mum!" Arti hadn't realised she'd been holding her breath while her mother spoke. She exhaled, hugging her mother and crying alongside her.

"And dad?"

"He'll come around, just give him time. Now, tell me about this Mohsin."

Jaipur 2017

"Bela, what have you done?" Her mother sat next to her, applying the cold compress to her forehead. She had been burning up with fever the last three days. In her delirium she had called out to Yusuf several times, enraging Amar even more.

He had paced up and down, unable to look at the bruise he'd inflicted on her when he'd struck her. Finally, her mother had ordered him to leave. Bela feared the worst now. Feared that he would find Yusuf and beat him senseless. She had no way to warn him, no way to tell him just what Amar was capable of.

"Maa, you have to get the phone off Amar. Please don't let him message Yusuf!"

"It's too late *beta*[16]. He's gone, and he's taken the phone with him."

"You have to warn Yusuf! You must tell him..." She sat up agitated, her mind filled with all kinds of horrors.

"Bela!" Her father's voice rang out from the other room. "No one will call or speak to that boy. You are to have no contact with him."

She sank back upon the bed and her eyes grew heavy once again. Where was Yusuf? Was he looking for her? Was he trying to call her?

Her mother smoothed her hair back from her forehead. She whispered to her, "I'll try and get a message across to him Bela. Give me his number and I'll find an excuse to leave the house. But you must rest now. Rest, get better. We'll find a way, okay? There's always a way..."

She fell asleep to her mother's ministrations, hope and terror bedfellows in her mind.

<u>**London 2017**</u>

The registered marriage had been quiet, with just her parents and his, in attendance. They planned to have a big *Nikaah*[17] ceremony later. Her nausea made it impossible for her to keep anything down, and it had been agreed to keep things small for the time being.

Mohsin's mother had hovered and clucked around her so much that her own mother had been pushed aside. Arti tried not to let her annoyance overshadow the happiness of the occasion, but somewhere, deep down, she felt a tinge of disquiet.

From the moment she had introduced Mohsin and his family to

hers, it seemed as though her parents were relegated to the background. However well-meaning and well intentioned his parents were, they were also overwhelming and overbearing. Mohsin seemed to go along with everything they said, and she often wondered if he had any opinion of his own.

"It's not that Arti. Ever since my *aapa*[18] got married and left home, all their hopes and dreams are tied up with me. If agreeing with them is all it takes to keep them happy, then why not? After all, they agreed to the most important thing - letting me marry you!"

Arti could not dispute this but wondered why it never occurred to him that she was the repository of all of her parents' hopes and dreams as well. In agreeing to marry him, she had all but turned those to ashes.

Dad had not taken to Mohsin. That was evident to her. He hadn't said much, but his silence spoke volumes.

"Why doesn't he like him mum?"

"Bela, that's not true. He just doesn't know him yet. Besides, most fathers react that way to their daughter's first serious love. My own dad took a long time to thaw."

That was stretching the truth and Arti knew it. Her grandad had always been very fond of dad.

Still, they would have to learn to rub along. In time, she knew, Mohsin would win a place in his heart. Till then, she would just have to put up with the silent animosity.

Jaipur 2017

"Where have you been Anju?" Baba's voice called out to her mother accusingly.

"I had to buy some groceries. There was no sugar, no rice..." As her mother reeled off a list of things she could see her father turn his attention back to the cricket match on the television.

Maa came over to her and put her hand on her forehead. "It's done," she said quietly.

Bela gripped her mother's hand.

"What did you say? What did he say?"

"Not now."

Her mother left her lying on the bed and took the bags to the kitchen.

Bela tossed and turned, worry coiling itself into a knot in her stomach. Finally, unable to bear it anymore, she stumbled out of bed and followed her mother.

"Maa?"

"Bela, I told him to stay away. I said it was for his best and for yours. I told him about the phone - not to answer it or engage in any conversation with Amar."

Bela leaned back on the wall and sighed.

"How did he respond?"

"I didn't give him any time to respond. The *Lala*[19] wanted the phone back and Rs,10 for the call on top of the grocery money." Her mother wiped the sweat off her brow with the edge of her sari *pallu*.[20]

"I'm sorry Maa. I'm sorry for all the trouble..." Bela started to weep.

Her mother drew her into her arms. "Shhhhh now... you're braver than this, surely? If your love is strong, it will withstand anything. If that boy loves you he will be patient. Bela, if anyone should be sorry, it should be us. Love is the most beautiful, most pure emotion there is, and to not allow two people to follow their hearts because they are of different faiths, that is a crime."

<u>London 2017</u>

"Well, look who has emerged from her self-imposed exile?" Shabnam enveloped her in a perfumed hug. "No replies to my texts, calls going unanswered, work telling me you're on sick leave. What the hell, girl? You had me real worried!"

"I'm married Shabz."

"What?! When? How? Why? Why didn't you tell me?"

"Shabz...Shabz...stop! It happened really quickly. What with the pregnancy and all, our parents felt it would be best."

"Your parents agreed?"

"Yes. Not happily, but yes."

"All of this in the last two weeks and nobody knows? You've been a real *chhupa rustam*[21]!"

Shabnam looked her over and then patted her hand.

"What's bothering you?"

"Nothing...I...I'm not sure..."

"Hang on! I think we need a few drinks first. Yeah, I know, I'll get you a club soda but I need a vino!"

They settled into a little booth and all her worries came pouring out.

"It's early days Shabz, but his mother is so bossy in every way. From what we eat, to when we eat to what I wear - she's full of 'suggestions'. The men say nothing. It's like Mohsin is another person around her. I've asked him time and again when we're moving to a place of our own but all he says is there's no rush. I'm feeling stifled and lonely. They are all very nice and I know it sounds like I'm complaining over nothing, but damn!"

"Okay, okay!" Shabnam started to laugh. "I think this maybe a case of 'Mother-in-Law-itis'! Couple that with your raging hormones, and it's no wonder you're climbing walls."

"That's not all."

"What else? She wants you to start crocheting?"

"No. Not crocheting. Praying."

Shabnam nearly choked on her wine.

"Yeah. She wants me to join her in her *namaaz*[22]. Says it'll be good for the baby, as of course, he will be brought up in their faith."

"Hey? I thought you said they were non-practising?"

"Liberal but not non-practising. Mohsin wants me to as well. He agrees that it will be good for the baby."

"Arti - this doesn't sound right. You need to get out and fast. Before you know it, she'll have you in a hijab and out of work."

"Don't know about the hijab, but they want me to take maternity leave pronto. The job is too stressful apparently!"

"I don't want to say, 'I told you so' but I did tell you so."

"It's not ALL bad Shabz. I'm just complaining to you because I can't to my parents. Mohsin is still as loving as ever, and his dad is really quite sweet and very respectful. It's just the mother. You know, you're probably right. It is probably 'Mother-in-law-itis'!" She laughed wryly.

"Yeah, but you watch it okay? First sign of any conversion stuff, get out of there! Run and don't look back."

"Shabz, don't be such a drama queen!"

Jaipur 2017

Bela tried hard to concentrate on the numbers before her, but her mind kept wandering to Yusuf. She hadn't heard from him in over three weeks. Had he given up on her already? He hadn't been to college either. Asking after him would put the both of them at unnecessary risk. At any rate, after her argument with Baba this morning, she had little stomach for any more drama.

"You have brought such shame upon our family name! Twenty years old and wandering the streets like a slut with that Muslim boy. I have a good mind to beat you with my stick till you see sense."

"Then do it Baba! And while you're at it, maybe have another think about who is bringing shame upon the family name. Me or your beloved Amar?"

"How dare you! How dare you raise your voice and talk to me in this manner?"

"Finding the truth unpalatable Baba? Let's see - who dropped out of school? Who joined a bunch of hoodlums that go around terrorising people into obedience? Who treats this house like a motel? Who contributes nothing to the household expenses yet walks around with his wallet stuffed with hundreds of Rupees? And you say *I* have brought shame upon you!"

Baba had raised his stick to hit her but instead of seeing her cower, he'd seen her move closer to him, as though daring him to do it. He'd clutched his chest then and retreated.

"Coward!" She'd muttered and walked out.

Life at home had become intolerable. Amar had taken to dropping in unannounced, more often than not. She knew he was checking up on her. She'd seen him follow her to college, turn up outside her student's house some evenings, known that he had rifled through her belongings in her absence. She was sick of being treated like a suspect and terrified that Yusuf had taken Maa's words to heart and truly abandoned her.

"Bela, wait up!" Roohi came running behind her. "Yaar[23], you walk too fast! Listen, I completely forgot but someone handed me a letter for you last week. It's been sitting in my bag, but it's not till I saw you just now that I remembered. Sorry *yaar*. It's sealed and everything. Here."

Bela took the envelope out of her hand. "Who gave this to you?"

"Some girl from Eco Honours. Said someone else had given it to her. Such cloak-and-dagger stuff. Are you like James Bond in hiding?"

Bela laughed and stuffed the envelope into her bag. She hung around and made conversation with Roohi, desperate to get to a quiet corner but aware she had to play it cool.

When she finally got away and sat under the peepul tree on the campus, her hands were shaking so badly, she had to take a minute to calm herself.

My darling Bela,

I know we've been found out. Your mother told me over the phone. The reason I haven't come to college is because I think your brother is following you and he may have informers among the students. He has sent me lots of threatening SMS. If we are spotted together, it could get really ugly. But, if we are careful, we could still meet. Remember our old meeting place? Meet me there on Wednesday, before your tuition class. I'll be waiting.

I love you.

Yusuf.

.   .   .

IT WAS THURSDAY TODAY, which meant she'd missed two Wednesdays. Would he have given up hope by now, or was it worth a try?

London 2017

Shabnam sat uncomfortably between Mohsin and his mother. There was no sign of Arti and she had been waiting over fifteen minutes. Finally, Arti emerged looking pale and worried.

"Oh my God! You're HUGE!!" Shabnam started to giggle. Arti threw her a desperate look and she stopped.

"It's so nice of you to drop by Shabnam."

"Well, I was concerned. Three months of no news so I took matters in my own hands, pulled a few strings, found your address and voila!"

"Ummm, thanks. I've just not had an easy pregnancy and the doctor has advised bed rest, so..."

"Would you like some tea?" Mohsin's mother asked. Her tone was cool as if willing her to say no.

"Oh yes please! The days are getting colder and a nice cuppa would be lovely." Shabnam smiled at her winningly.

"So, when is the baby due?"

"December." Mohsin answered.

"I'm a December baby! Sagittarians are really lucky people. You'll see. This baby will bring you a lot of luck too."

"We don't believe in all that astrological nonsense. Allah's will is our will."

"Yeah, sure. I mean, all I meant was..." Shabnam ran out of words.

Mohsin's phone buzzed and he walked out of the room to take the call.

"Arti, what the heck is going on?" Shabnam whispered.

"Shabz, contact my parents. Tell them to get me out of here. Please...I beg you..." Arti whispered back.

"Here is the tea. I've brought some digestives too. You look a bit hungry to me Shabnam."

Arti sank back into a listless silence. Her mother-in-law planted herself between them.

"Wow, thanks! How did you guess?"

"I am a good judge of character."

She was given the once over once again. Shabnam suppressed her shudder, wondering if she'd wandered into some kind of sinister soap opera. Except that her friend was no actress and this was no fiction designed to keep bored housewives entertained.

"Arti, when are you coming back to work then?"

"She's not." Mohsin sauntered in. "Not that it's anyone's business but Arti will have her hands full with the baby. Besides, the women in our household don't work. We are more than capable of taking care of them."

"What if she wants to work?"

"Do you, my darling?" Mohsin leaned over and reached for Arti's hand.

"N...no...no...of course not."

Shabnam had seen enough. She got up abruptly.

"I have to go. Thank you for your hospitality and sorry for barging in unannounced."

She hugged Arti.

"I'll see you soon, okay?"

"I don't think that is a good idea. Arti needs her rest and we are trying to keep visitors to a minimum. You can come by after the baby is born."

The mother-in-law had made it clear she was not welcome anymore.

She'd see about that.

Jaipur 2017

Three months of dodging her brother and his friends, three months of putting up with her father's injured silences and reassuring her mother that she was fine. Three months of plotting and planning different venues so that they could meet undetected. Three months of thinking of what was really important to her and how to proceed.

"Bela, once the exams are done, no more college and no more communication. What will we do then?"

"Yusuf, I have given it a lot of thought, and I think we are left with no choice but to elope."

In the silence that followed, Bela took his hand in hers and gave it a reassuring squeeze.

"Maa will understand. As for Baba and Amar, it has become obvious to me that my happiness and wellbeing is not something either of them cares about. So, why should I bother about them?"

They sat together in a quiet corner of the college campus, behind the auditorium.

"Next week, after the last exam, I will meet you at the Railway station. We'll buy tickets for Delhi. My *masi* [24]lives there. She will help us. I have already written and asked, and she has said yes. Just think - this time next week we will be husband and wife!"

Bela beamed at him. Once her mind had been made up, all doubts had fallen away. Yusuf had more than proven his love, taking chance upon chance to see her. He had waited patiently for two weeks for her to appear, never once giving up on her. If he was willing to risk his life for her, then she was willing to risk her family's ire for him.

"Are you sure about this? You know you will be marrying an unemployed Muslim man with no money, no house and parents, and siblings to support. This isn't a joke Bela. I know I've suggested eloping before, but I want you to think carefully about this."

"What do you think I've been doing these past few months? And you're not exactly winning the lottery with me. I will be unemployed too. Plus, you'll have my crazy brother to contend with. I think it's a fair trade off."

They both started to laugh. In that Autumnal sunshine, everything seemed possible and the future, if not assured, then at the very least, not frightening.

· · ·

<u>London 2017</u>

She wanted to call it an intervention. It had taken her weeks and all her skills of persuasion to make Arti's father believe that his daughter truly needed his help.

"She allowed us to be insulted and thrown out of that house. Her mother-in-law said all sorts of nasty things to us. Mohsin manhandled me and Arti just stood by and watched. How could she?"

"Mr Jain, you have to understand, Arti is being put under a tremendous amount of pressure. I'm not sure what is going on behind the scenes, but don't you find it odd that your daughter, a girl who you've raised and loved for twenty five years, has changed so dramatically in the last six months?"

"Puneet, listen to her. I've been telling you all along that something is wrong. They are manipulating her somehow. We have to help her. Even if it means listening to that wretched woman's insults!"

Arti's mother reminded her of Arti. She had the same gamine charm along with the spunk that had first drawn her to Arti when they'd met at a conference. Her father had a steadfastness and a stubbornness, the same qualities that had propelled Arti headlong into her relationship with Mohsin. How could things have gone so wrong for her friend? What had they done to subdue her into submission?

An intervention was in order. They would turn up in the evening and demand to see Arti. They'd get her out of that house on some pretext or the other. Then, they'd get the truth out of her. If, as she suspected, things were rotten to the core, then Arti would have to make a clean break. There was no other way.

She gnawed at her thumbnail in the back of the car as they navigated the rush hour traffic towards Arti's in laws' home. She had no doubt that Arti was in trouble and they had to rescue her somehow. She only hoped that it could be done with minimum fuss. Her own problematic past and fractured relationship with her family kept playing out in her mind. Despite all her protestations, she missed them and would give anything to have them back in her life. Anything except give up Mark.

The house looked strangely quiet. They rang the bell, rapped on the front door and called out.

"Maybe they are all out?" Arti's mother remarked, her nervousness apparent.

Shabnam rang the doorbell again. The neighbour, an elderly Asian lady came outside.

"There is no one in that house."

"Are they away?" Shabnam asked.

"No. They sold the house about ten days ago."

"Do you know where they went? A forwarding address perhaps?"

"No. They didn't really mingle with us. I heard the young woman, the pregnant one, screaming the other day. I went to enquire, and they turned me away quite rudely."

Arti's father slumped onto the ground.

"My child" he whispered. "What have they done to my child?"

Jaipur 2017

Bela waited and waited. The railway platform filled and emptied with each passing train. She held the two tickets in her hands, her mind filling with doubts that she shooed away just as quickly. Yusuf would come. He would come. They would go to Delhi. They would get married. He would not betray her. He could not betray her.

Their train arrived.

Their train left.

Three hours of waiting finally gave Bela her answer.

She walked home, dry eyed. Tears were of no use to her now. Something inside her had hardened. Love had been a silly game that she had played and lost. More the fool her! Nothing would rob her of her dignity. Not Amar, not her father, not Yusuf. Men who treated her like a burden, a nuisance, a commodity.

"Bela, *beti!*" Her mother rushed to embrace her. "I've been so worried! Where were you?"

Numb and exhausted, she tuned her mother out. She wanted to

lie down and sleep. Enter a blessed oblivion where hurt and betrayal could be temporarily banished.

"Bela!!" Her mother shook her. "Are you listening? The police have taken Amar away. He's done something bad, something really bad! Your baba has gone to the police station."

"What has he done?" Bela asked, disinterested, wanting to get away from everything and everyone.

"He has killed a boy! They say he filmed it and put it on something...something...Tee...Twee..."

"Twitter?"

"Yes...that... Bela, it is on the news...I can't watch it *beti*. It's too horrible...how could he? What will happen to him now?"

Automaton like, Bela turned the television on to the news channel.

There he was - Amar, holding a can of kerosene in his hand, his eyes maniacal, laughing, gesturing at the man bound and gagged behind him. Then he poured the kerosene all over the man, shouting, gesticulating, drenching the shaking man. Then he lit a match and threw it at the man who lit up immediately. There was no volume to the video. It had been edited out to contain the distress it could cause to the viewers.

The primal scream that escaped her contained enough anguish to drown out everything else. She sunk to her knees, a white-hot agony coursing through her, turning her insides molten.

Yusuf burning to death.

Yusuf burning.

Yusuf.

Zindagi Ek sawal hai Jis ka jawab maut hai,
maut Bhi Ek sawal hai Jis ka jawab Kuch Nahi.[25]

8

THE UNLIKELY CASANOVA

He sat looking into his glass of amber liquid, a smile hovering on his lips. The lone ice cube in there was melting rapidly, quite unlike his latest conquest. The ice maiden. It had taken a while with her. And yet, her defeat, when it came, was sudden and unequivocal. Another one that had bitten the dust, grovelled at his feet, expecting a reciprocal love, aghast when it was not returned. He dipped a finger into his glass, swirling the cube, watching it disperse. She had been the latest in his long line of acquisitions. Women, he had always known and feared, were out of his league. Women, who previously would have barely given him a second glance, except that now, they did.

Words were his weapons. Weapons that wreaked destruction stealthily. This had never been open warfare. It had been a subtle seduction. A beguiling of the senses. A promise of pleasure, with a subtext of pain. He stalked them covertly at first, then brazenly. Showering them with images. Showing them what was lacking in their lives. The lacunae that he could fill. That he would fill, if only they would give him a chance. They would laugh at him at first. Then be intrigued. Then flattered. Till finally, they could not move, without a thought of him filling every vacant moment of their vacant lives.

Like moths, they would draw nearer and nearer to their own destruction, wilfully abandoning all thoughts of self-preservation. He was the cauldron into which all their desires would subsume.

It was a matter of finding the chink. The Achilles heel that every single one of them possessed. With some, it was loneliness, with others it was the lack of love, of sex, of affection, and with others still, it was simply boredom and ennui. It took him very little time to figure out what their compulsions were. Then he worked on them, like a Master violinist working his strings, tautening the tension, till they could take no more, and shivering with delicious anticipation, they would yield to him. At that point, he would walk away. The thrill was in the chase, not in the victory. The game would be over for him.

She had been different, he thought. A challenge. One that could match him, word for word, sabre thrust for sabre thrust. It had been his turn to be intrigued. Even as he had spun his web of words around her, he had felt himself getting caught up in it too. Entangled in emotions that he had no business entertaining. For a brief time he had wondered if he had finally found love, found 'the one'. In the end, however, she was much like the others. Promising to give it all up for him. For a chance to be held in his arms. His nose had puckered at the predictability of it all.

He had offered her advice. Sage, solemn advice. To seek counsel. To redress the wrongs in her relationship. He did not figure in her future, he calmly informed her. He had watched her distress with a disembodied disenchantment. And it had occurred to him, that he simply did not care.

With a quick glug, he downed his whiskey. The room around him blurred and swayed a little. With a groan, he heaved himself out of his chair, and walked unsteadily to his bed. Thoughts and words coalesced in his mind as he lowered himself onto the mattress. He drew the sheet up to his chin, shivering unaccountably in the heat. His hand reached over to the other side of the bed. No one. There never was. There probably never would be.

Game over.

9

SWAMI CLAUS

I am claustrophobic. Always have been. Perhaps the last time I felt safe in an enclosed space it was my mother's womb. Perhaps.

So, you see, lying here in this tunnel with nothing but a dead body for company must be the Almighty's idea of an almighty joke. A joke that has set my heart galloping, turned my skin clammy and had a scream stuck in my throat for far too many hours.

When the going is good, one rarely sits back to think of the whys and the wherefores. It's when things turn sour that your mind tries to unravel the sequence of events that led to the moment of downfall. And so, my mind, of its own volition, has decided to travel back in time.

I MUST HAVE BEEN five when I was first introduced to the Swami. I flew half way across the world with my hippie parents to meet a jolly, bearded man in white robes who laughed a lot.

"Is that God?" I asked my mother.

"No silly, that is the Swami."

How or why I started to confuse the Swami with Santa Claus I do not know. After all, Santa lived in the North Pole and wore red. He rode a sleigh and brought presents for good children at Christmas. The Swami lived in India, wore white and never, to my recollection, ever handed out any presents. The only thing they had in common was their beards. Although, while Santa's beard was snowy white and bushy, Swami's was jet black, wispy and long. As long as the hair on his head.

It was the era of 'finding oneself' and my parents went looking for themselves in an Ashram in India. California was a hub of hedonism and excess. They wanted a simpler living, a connection to the earth and their fellow beings. The Swami's ashram offered them a sort of refuge. You grew your own vegetables, lived dormitory style with other residents or in tiny cottages with your families, prayed together, cleaned together, ate together. Your children ran barefoot and happy in the yard and life was easy for the two months you could afford to escape for.

My memories of that time are hazy at best. What I do remember is the heat, the many games of hide and seek, and the mangoes. Ripe, sweet, juicy, delicious. As a mixed race child, my olive skin would turn as dark as the native children but my blue eyes would stand out in stark contrast, setting me apart, positioning me right at the top of the hierarchical totem pole. I would get the pick of the mangoes.

Returning to America was always a wrench. Suddenly, even the most laid-back Californian ways would seem restrictive and stifling. It would take weeks for us to readjust ourselves. Weeks that we would spend lying awake at night or sniping at each other in the day.

When I was eight my parents divorced. It had been a long time coming. My father promptly took off and joined a commune. Mum was left to take care of me, pay the bills and the substantial mortgage my father had saddled her with. There was no help forthcoming from her parents. They had given up on her the day she'd insisted on marrying 'that hippie loser' my father had been. Not even his abandonment of her would change their minds.

We struggled along for a few months, till one day, in a fit of pique, Mum decided she'd had enough. We sold everything within a month and decided to move continents, although I didn't have much say in the decision-making process.

That is how I found myself living permanently in the Swami's ashram.

"*Didi*[1], your eyes are so blue." Aditi says.

"Mmmm-hmm."

"Yet, you speak Hindi so well."

"What do the colour of my eyes have to do with speaking Hindi?"

That shuts her up. I know she is trying to probe my antecedents. They have been trying for years. I like to keep an air of mystery about me. You don't ascend the greasy pole of power by blabbing to all and sundry.

"When are the new recruits arriving?"

"Tomorrow *didi*. Don't worry, their rooms are all cleaned and ready for them. I even have copies of the tasks sheet printed out."

I nod my approval. Aditi is efficient, I will give her that.

"Will Swami *ji* be speaking tomorrow?"

"I don't know yet. I will let you know after our meeting."

I hurry out of the room. There are many jobs to be done, and as I am the overseer of most, I cannot afford to slacken my pace.

After lunch I retire to my bungalow for a short siesta. I rarely sleep in the afternoons. This is my time to recharge and think through the day's events and the evening's program. It is also my time to plan and strategise. There are enough usurpers waiting to topple me but I am nothing if not tenacious.

Is it my imagination or is the body beginning to smell? How long have I been here? How much longer must I stay?

"LOLITA, Swami wants to talk to you this evening."

Mum was folding our clothes as she announced this to me. We had been living in the ashram for two years now. At twelve I had just entered my gawky, pre-teenage phase. I was all awkward limbs, big nose, under developed bosom and over developed intellect.

"What about?"

I had had nothing to do with the Swami until now. He was a distant, father like figure who conducted our evening meditation sessions which I mostly day dreamed my way through. His discourses were for the adults and the meetings in his bungalow only for the inner circle. This much I had ascertained in my two years.

My mother did not belong to the inner circle, much as she yearned to. It was her life's ambition to become a part of the Swami's management team. Yet, for no apparent reason, she remained on the outside.

"It's because I'm half caste. I'm a mongrel. I'm not pure enough."

She moaned about this often enough for me, disinterested as I was in our gene pool, to ask her what that meant.

"My father, your grandfather, is Indian. But he is a Kenyan Indian, so not Indian enough for the Swami. And your grandmother is of German descent. I am mixed blood. Swami likes his team to be pure blood. I am certain that is why I am not included."

I nodded sympathetically and promptly forgot our conversation. It was only later, much much later, that I came to realise how wrong she was.

The Swami wanted people who were clever with money, savvy with marketing and ruthless with power, to be in his inner circle. My mother was none of these and never would be. What she was, was desperate.

~

DECOMPOSING. *Putrefying. Rotting. Crumbling. Decaying.*

~

He is but a shadow of the man he used to be. Those powerful arms have shrunk to nothing. The beard is greying and matted, the eyes listless, the speech confused. A little saliva dribbles out from the side of his mouth and I watch it make its way into his beard. I make no attempt to dab at it. He looks at me pleadingly.

"L...L..Lalita?"

"Swami, I will pass your message on to the new recruits. You need not worry yourself about it. All will be done according to your will. You just need to sign this here."

His hand shakes as he attempts a signature at the bottom of the page.

"M...m...my med...medicine?"

"Ah, of course."

Quick as a flash I take the needle out of my bag. It is ready to go. I plunge it into his upper arm, ignoring his wince. His pain is of no concern to me.

In 1955, Vladimir Nabokov wrote a book called Lolita.

Was I named after her? The precocious girl lusted after by the vile old man? My mother died before I could get any answers from her. My father I never saw again. Was their naming of me an irony under the influence of heaven-knows-what drugs or a prescience of what would come later?

As my mother accompanied me to the Swami's bungalow that evening, I was mildly irritated at having to miss my Scrabble game with Hari. He was the only one smart enough to beat me and our competition had been going strong the last couple of weeks. The best of fifteen we had decided. Fifteen games had been won and lost but we kept going. Madly in thrall with the words we could create, the scores we could generate and the recognition of a worthy adversary.

"You can send her in." The sentry at the door was one of the Swami's inner circle.

"I'd like to go in too." Ma never failed to pass on an opportunity to be near the Swami.

"Those are the instructions."

I looked between the man and my mother and saw the defeat written on her face as she nodded her acquiescence.

I was ushered into the sitting room of the Swami. It was early evening and the sun was close to setting. Ordinarily all the windows would be opened to let the day's heat out and the cool evening breeze in. Here, the windows were shut, and the curtains drawn. There was an air of hush in the room as though every noise was absorbed, muffled and contained within. There were incense sticks placed in the four corners and the heady perfume of sandalwood permeated the atmosphere.

The Swami himself sat on a single white, gilt edged settee that resembled a throne. This was the royal inner chamber. A chamber filled with white and gold. A chamber of power, authority and entitlement. A chamber my mother yearned for an entree to. A chamber that I had been invited into. All at once I felt humbled and privileged.

He motioned to me to come to him and indicated that I sit at his feet. I stared up at him mesmerised. There was a mole on his upper right cheek with a hair that protruded from it. His lips were thin but beautifully shaped. His teeth were even and white, and his smile, loving and benevolent. But it was his eyes, those liquid black pools of intensity that drew you to him, bending your will to his, willing you to surrender, yield, capitulate.

THE TUNNEL HAD BEEN a means to an end. Its existence was known only to a few. The inner circle had diminished over the years. After all, a secret is no longer a secret when it becomes the property of more than one. I was the architect of the tunnel. Not physically of course, but in my vision and in the execution. It was a means to <u>and</u> a getaway from. Doubly ironic then that I find myself trapped in it today.

"The Swami says that there is no such thing as control. All we have is the illusion of control. We think that by educating ourselves, by getting good jobs, by buying houses and cars, by marrying well and having children, we are controlling our destinies. Yet, how many of us come up against random events like unexpected accidents, unforeseen deaths, catastrophic natural disasters? Can we predict these? Can we control them? No! It takes just a moment to turn our well-organised, on track, 'in control' lives upside down. That is why it is important to believe in the Divine order. The plan that the Almighty executes on our behalf..."

I look at the audience of more than a thousand people spread out in front of me. Some are our local residents, but most have come from various corners of the world to listen to the Swami's message. Are they feeling cheated that it is his deputy that delivers it to them instead? My voice is calm and measured, fine-tuned to public speaking, an art I have honed over the years. It seems to be working.

None of what I am delivering as a speech today has come from the Swami recently. He is incapable of stringing a sentence together let alone any words of wisdom. What I have done is create a patchwork of speeches taken from his earlier communiques. A patchwork of wisdom delivered piecemeal to gullible followers.

My speech ends, and the floor is opened to questions.

"When will we see the Swami?"

"Why does the Swami not speak anymore?"

"I have come all the way from Holland to touch the Swami's feet and receive his blessings. Where is he?"

I answer patiently.

"As we have posted on the website and said to many of you personally, the Swami is in a state of '*maun vrat*'.[2] This is a state of silence and solitude. He speaks to no one and interacts with just a few of us. He is ascending to a higher spiritual plane, one where all material attachments will gradually fall away. He is in communication with the Divine."

An awed silence descends upon the audience. When you have voluntarily chosen to sip from the chalice of deception, a dash of hokum moonshine is gulped down just as easily.

THE SWAMI DIDN'T GIVE. He took away. He took my innocence, he took my virginity and he took my trust.

My mother rocked me backwards and forwards, her face awash with tears. She had bathed me, tended to my wounds and then taken me into her embrace.

"Loli, you understand that we cannot say anything? No one will believe us. He is too well respected and too powerful. We will be cast out. Then where will we go? No one will believe us."

She kept repeating herself, but I had tuned her out long ago. It was evident to me that she was powerless. A fragile woman subject to the whims and fancies of the world. A woman incapable of protecting her child. A woman incapable of standing up to anyone. A weak, feeble, useless woman.

I curled myself into a ball on the bed. She kept talking, stroking my back.

"I'll keep you away from him. Far far away. We'll stay here but I will never take you back to that house. I won't allow him to touch you again."

I wondered if she knew how false her platitudes sounded.

That night I had my first nightmare. I was being suffocated. Someone was trying to kill me. I was in a tunnel trying to run away but my feet kept sinking into a swamp. I was drowning in the swamp. Unable to breathe, unable to scream. I woke up shaking, my entire body drenched in sweat, a silent scream caught in my throat, my heart thudding so loudly that I felt it would jump right out of my chest.

It was a nightmare that would recur my entire life.

IN MY LIVING nightmare I'm lying next to the Swami's body. His eyes stare at me accusingly in the dark, as though all of this is my fault. He is long gone but his accusation hovers in the air. Is <u>all</u> of it my fault, I wonder. Did I set the ball of destruction rolling? Did I, somehow, subconsciously, want it all to fail? Was this the revenge that I exacted for the loss of my innocence? A revenge that would boomerang back on me?

HARI HELPS me move him to the bed. The Swami is light enough for us to manage between us.

"Lolita, he's not looking good. Maybe we should get a doctor in?"

"No! No doctors. He'll be fine. I'll just up the dose."

"What if he dies? Have you thought of that? What if the worst happens?"

"Hari, I'm not stupid. Of course, I've thought of it. I just need to get my hands on the deeds of the land and transfer them over to us. Then if he dies, he dies. He'll be declared a saint. People will flood this Ashram, and we will let them canonise him and throw more money at us. Once the hoopla dies down, we can make our escape."

"Lols, aren't you worried at all?"

"Hari, you, of all people, should know that worry accomplishes nothing. When we embarked upon this plan, we never imagined we'd get this far. Now that we have, we can't let worry or cowardice stop us."

"When did you become this hard Lols?"

SCRABBLE SAVED me from going mad. Hari too. Maybe even at the age of thirteen he sensed that all was not right with me. He never gave up on me though. He would turn up every day, Scrabble board in hand, willing me to play him. My mother would turn him away, saying I was not 'well enough'. One day, out of spite, I said I was well enough and stomped out with him.

It took many months before he broached the subject.

"Lolita, do you go to see the Swami every week?"

I stiffened in fear. How did he know? He placed his hand upon mine.

"You're not the first. He likes young girls. Always has. The moment you develop some more," his cheeks reddened as he looked at my flat chest, "he will lose interest and look elsewhere."

"How do you know this, and how did I not?"

"Oh, everyone knows it. It's the price we pay for living here."

"We? What price have you paid?"

Hari looked at the tile in his hand and turned it over.

"Suresh sir, the Swami's deputy, has been abusing me since I was seven."

I sat in appalled silence. Our parents, our guardians, our so-called protectors were letting this happen to us under the guise of spirituality and redemption?

Hari looked at me and shrugged. "It's okay. I'm used to it now. My parents sold all their assets to move here. They gave everything to the Ashram. We have nowhere to go either. They say it is a small price to pay for security. There will come a time when he will tire of me and I will be free."

An idea took shape in my mind then. An idea that would eventually take us down some very dark alleyways. But an idea that would make sure that someday we would be the ones holding the reins of power. That no one would ever be able to treat us as puppets to use, abuse and discard at will.

It has to be over ten hours now. Where is Hari? Day must have broken, and they must be missing us now. What must they be thinking? I wish I had my watch. I turn my face away from the Swami's body. There is no comfortable way to sit in here, so I must keep lying down. I could try and creep towards the exit but what good will that do? Hari should have come hours ago. Has something happened to him?

THE SWAMI BEGAN to buy into his own hype. He started to believe the sycophants who said he was omnipotent and omniscient. With such arrogance it was easy to dismiss the two teenagers that were inveigling their way into the sanctum sanctorum.

I thought back to those days and a thrill went through me again. Whatever it takes, we had vowed. Flattery, seduction, persuasion, deception. We would employ any and every means to gain their trust. After all, the best way to take down an enemy is from within, isn't it?

It took years. A slow chipping away at their distrust, performing as minions, becoming indispensable, taking on the uglier tasks. Letting ourselves be used, letting ourselves learn the secrets of these powerful people. Burrowing our way in - slowly, cautiously but steadily. Years of dismantling the Swami's set up and installing our own in its place.

What neither of us had anticipated was that over the course of time, we would become the very thing that we despised.

"SIGN HERE, OLD MAN!"

A moment of lucidity and he turns his head away. His hands lie slack by his side. I can no more will him to sign than get a petulant child to share its sweets.

He looks up at me, a glimmer of understanding in his eyes.

"Y...y...you really hate me, no?"

I laugh at him then.

"Yes, your darling Lalita, your devoted follower, your trusted deputy really hates you Swami *ji*!"

I look at his diminished form sitting on that yellowing throne.

"What you did to me all those years ago in this very room...what you have done to all those children ... what you have made *me* do - pimp and procure for you...did you think I did all of it willingly? Did you think I was so blind in my faith that I accepted all your evil ways as the ways of the Divine? Do you think I even believe in the Divine after having seen you corrupt everyone and everything around you? Think again, old man!"

"Look around you. Who do you have? Who can you trust? There's just Hari and me. We have isolated you, just as we meant to. Now, you are at our mercy. How does that feel? Tell you what, you ridiculous degenerate Swami-of-nothing, I may not believe in the Divine, but I most certainly believe in Karma!"

Karma. *That word taunts me. I was no better than the Swami. All those strong-arm tactics with vulnerable families, all those bribes given and taken, all those favours called in, but worst of all, all those children that I led willingly, knowingly into the arms of their abusers.*

What was my Karma then? And how was I going to pay?

Comfort eating, a concept I had no idea of at fourteen, but one that Ma started to indulge in frequently. I saw her balloon before my very eyes.

"Ma, another box of *barfi*[3]? What is wrong with you?"

"Loli, you know I like my sweets."

She had always had a sweet tooth but now it was out of control. I watched her struggle to mop the floor of our tiny cottage, taking frequent breaks, wheezing as she got back on her haunches. I heard her waking up at 3am to go and forage in the kitchen for some munchies. I saw her turn from a svelte, attractive woman in her forties into a fat, ugly replica of her former self.

"I don't know what's happening to her Hari. Every time I turn around she is stuffing her face."

"She's drowning her sorrows in food Lols. I guess she feels guilty and doesn't know who to turn to."

"What about your parents? Did they do the same?"

"Oh no. They turned even more religious, if that is possible. They threw themselves into all sorts of community projects. They volunteered in nearly every society we have. Now, my father heads the education committee and my mother leads the prayer group."

"Do they ever ask you about...about...?"

"No, Lols. Their existence and progress within this community hinges on turning a blind eye. Why would they?"

What a strange world we were living in. On the outside it seemed like Utopia. People co-existing in spiritual harmony. No colour, no creed, no caste. Everyone equal to the other. Each on a journey of discovery. The Swami's perfect world. One that he held up as an example to the rest of the world. One that he lured susceptible and preferably rich people to join.

And yet.

"Lols, enough! We need to get a doctor in. We can't leave him like this."

The Swami was having an epileptic seizure. I had put a cloth between his teeth while he jerked and spasmed on the floor.

"It will pass Hari. Look, I've finally managed to get the code to the safe. We have to hurry. I don't think he's got a lot of time left."

"Lols! Look at me. This is not right. It's inhumane."

I stopped my search and looked Hari square in the face.

"And how is Hans?"

He took a step back.

"What does this have to do with Hans?"

"Everything, doesn't it?"

Hans - tanned, tall, blonde, handsome new recruit. Hans - Hari's latest paramour.

"Just how much have you told him Hari?"

"I've told him nothing Lols. Nothing except that the Swami isn't keeping too well."

"And I suppose your precious Hans has suggested bringing a

doctor in? How do you suppose we'll explain the needle marks on his arms or the bed sores on his back or the fact that he has received no medical attention at all in the last three years, although clearly he requires it? Hmmm? Come on, tell me how?"

He mumbled something.

"What did you say? Speak up!"

"I said Lols, there are ways. We can pay the doctor to keep mum, can't we? We've done it before...when that boy nearly bled to death...remember?"

I remembered, even though I didn't want to. There were things in my past I wished I could obliterate.

"Why this sudden crisis of conscience? All this self-flagellation? You know what you signed up for. What do you care if this despicable bastard lives or dies?"

THE AIR IS SO stale in here, I feel like I'm suffocating. All at once, my old nightmare resurfaces, and my body begins to tremble. I can no longer distinguish between reality and fantasy. I can no longer tell whether I am awake, asleep or dying. The Swami has stiffened with rigor mortis and whilst my body shakes in terror, his lies motionless in necrosis.

THE TUNNEL HAD BEEN my idea. Too many leaks had happened. It was unsafe bringing the children to the Swami as we used to before. In the age of the internet and social media, news travelled faster than light. So, we built a tunnel.

"Crouching height only. It must be, so no adults can take it upon themselves to enter or investigate."

"Lalita, I like the idea, but who will build this tunnel?"

"Swami *ji* you leave all that to me. I will find the labour and I'll make sure they never speak of it to anyone. Besides, we must have an exit route for you, just in case things go wrong. The tunnel will prong out and lead to the fields at the back of the Ashram. We will stash a getaway car there with all the necessary documents if you need to flee the country."

"Such a clever girl!"

The Swami had kissed my forehead and I had barely managed to suppress my shudder.

"You will have to crawl out but if it ever comes to it, I think that will be the least of our worries."

Even as I had planned and plotted, my mother had lain dying with congestive heart failure. Severely diabetic, morbidly obese, racked with guilt, she had speeded up her own demise. What she felt about my entree into the Swami's upper echelons, I never found out. We had stopped speaking a long time ago.

HE MUST HAVE DIED while Hari and I argued. Slipped away so quietly that we didn't even notice. It was only when the tray crashed to the floor that we looked up to see Aditi standing in the doorway.

She was looking down at the Swami's body in horror. She looked up at us, at the mess in the room and comprehension started to dawn on her face.

"Grab her Hari," I whispered, "Quick!"

He had his hand on her mouth before she could scream, dragging her into the room.

Damn it all to Hell! Which one of us had left the door unlocked? Normally one of us would go and collect the Swami's tray from her. No one was allowed access into this room. We must have missed her knocking and she had walked in on us.

She was struggling in Hari's arms.

"Aditi, shhhhh, calm down. Listen to me. Just listen!"

Her eyes were wide with shock as I tried to soothe her with my words.

"This is not what you're thinking... it's not what it looks like... The Swami has been unwell. He wanted me to look for some documents he had misplaced and while Hari and I were looking, he must have collapsed..."

The cloth I had placed in his mouth to prevent him from biting down on his tongue seemed to bely my version of events. Aditi looked at it, then looked at me; disbelieving, incredulous.

She bit down hard on Hari's hand and shoved him aside, trying to escape. I grabbed the heavy ashtray from the Swami's desk and threw it at her head in an attempt to stop her. As it connected I heard a sharp crack. She fell to the floor clutching her head, moaning. Blood gushed out of the wound in spurts.

Already she was trying to get back on her feet, scrambling to get away from us. I picked up the ashtray from the floor beside her and hit her repeatedly till she stopped moving.

Hari stood silent holding his bleeding hand. There was blood everywhere. His, hers, maybe even mine. A veritable bloodbath.

HE HAD PROMISED to clean it all up. Promised that he'd come get me once he'd disposed of her body. Told me to stay hidden with the Swami till it was time to tell the world. Promised me that all would be well. We had planned for this day. Not quite in this manner, but everything was in its place, wasn't it?

I have lost all sense of time in here. It could be a few hours, a few days or even a few weeks. All I know is that Hari has not come to get me. I am running out of patience. I must find out what has happened, even if it means arrest and imprisonment.

I start to crawl back towards the entrance of the tunnel. I remember Hari pulling the Swami's body in here, and I crouching down behind them, following in the belief that it would only be a few hours of discomfort.

I crawl, scraping my elbows and knees, my breath ragged and thin. I crawl, reliving the nightmare of my dreams. There is no light and I only have a vague sense of direction. I keep crawling till I hit a wall. Is it a wall? I probe at it with my hands and feel the uneven surface of the bricks.

Bricks? There should have been a wooden door that opened out behind the Swami's throne. Confused, I crawl backwards. There is another exit. The one I used to bring the children in from.

I contort my body, turning it to face the other direction. There is an urgency to my movements now, a panic that is threatening to derail me. I come upon the Swami's body and climb over it, kicking at it as I do.

I crouch now, my back bent into a painful C. I feel the the walls of the tunnel closing in on me and banishing all thought, propel myself forward rapidly. Once again I hit a barrier. Bricks.

I try and remember where the tunnel forked out. If only I could get outside. If only I could breathe in a fresh lungful of air. Maddened, blinded, lost, I keep crawling, crouching, feeling, falling. Like a maze with no end, I keep hitting brick walls. I no longer know where I am and which wall I have come upon.

I hit at them all, pounding with all my might. I yell but the yells only rebound on me. I scream till my throat is raw. I claw at the bricks till my fingers bleed. I cry till I have no tears left.

Then I fall silent.

In that rotting, suffocating, noxious hellhole I hear distant laughter. And I know.

Karma has ridden in on her chariot.

10

UGLY

Ramesh

The sound of the *shehnai*[1] is still reverberating in my head. I am a little drunk.

She sits, all demure, amongst the flower petals scattered on the bed. Her sari is a bright fuchsia that makes my eyes hurt. I try to recall what she looks like, but for the life of me, cannot.

"You okay?" I slur at her.

She nods imperceptibly.

I pull the heavy flowered head dress off impatiently. The shoes come off next sending a fetid odour up in the air. Damn *mojris*[2]! I strip down to my vest and shorts leaving the shiny clothes in a heap on the floor. I turn to face her. She hasn't stirred. What was I hoping to see? Kimi Katkar, my hot Hindi film crush, languishing in a bikini? I snort at the thought and she cocks her head slightly.

"You want some milk?" I offer ungraciously. The milk is for me. For my virility. But one has to start somewhere.

She demurs. Is she dumb? She hasn't said a word yet.

I peer at her uncertainly.

"Have you eaten?"

I can remember someone placing a common plate with all the

wedding food on it for us to share. One *thaali*[3] to signify a common future, an unbreakable bond. I was too inebriated to eat much, and I cannot recall if she did.

"*Haan ji*[4]." She answers in the affirmative, a low soft yes that I barely catch.

My relief is palpable. I drink the milk in quick gulps.

I wipe my mouth with the back of my hand and advance towards her.

I touch her on the shoulder and feel her tremble. My erection surprises me with its vigour. I yank the veil off her and stare at the face of my wife. Her features are a blur, her startled gaze excites me strangely. I tug and tear at her clothes, no longer bothering with any preliminaries. She lies under me submissive and scared. Her breasts are small. Too small. But I don't care. I touch her and rub her in a frenzy. Then I push her legs open with my knee and enter her forcibly. There is some resistance, but I push in viciously. And suddenly I am there. Paradise. Warm, soft, inviting. I ignore her cries as I push and push, chasing my own crazy rhythm. The crescendo hears me moan so loudly that I drown out her sobs. Then I retreat. I wipe myself with the edge of her sari. I turn my back to her and fall into a deep slumber.

Sujata

I lie there listening to the cadence of his snores. They start out softly, then get louder and louder till I feel the roof will cave in...then they settle into a low wheezy whistle. I listen to the rustling of the leaves outside. I concentrate on the drip of the tap in the toilet. Anything to take my mind off the pain and humiliation of my wedding night. I hurt everywhere. Everywhere that he pinched and squeezed and bit. I feel a burning sensation between my legs, and a wetness I dare not examine for fear of what I'll see. I hurt everywhere, but there is a dull pain in my heart. A lump in my throat that will not go away. So, I push it deep down, till it doesn't threaten to burst out into uncontrollable tears. I lie still and wait for the morning to arrive.

The first morning of the first day of my life as the wife of Ramesh Singh Ghaturia.

As the early rays of sunshine filter through the dirty curtains, I slip out of bed quietly. I wash and change hastily, scrubbing at the blood vigorously. The sheets will have to be washed. My husband will have to be fed. The house will have to be cleaned. My mental list gets longer as I limp towards the bed.

Suddenly I catch my breath. His supine face is bathed in the glow of the morning sunshine. He is so incredibly handsome. That aquiline nose, those grey eyes still shut in sleep, that milky complexion. No wonder my aunts had twittered at my luck.

"*Arré*[5], it's a good thing he didn't ask to see *your* face, or he might have changed his mind! Your dowry is making it all worthwhile. Or who would marry you? Twenty eight, uneducated, just a maid at some memsahib's house..." My father had winked conspiratorially at me. We had long since learned to ignore their taunts.

I bite back a sob at the thought of *Paa*. His love was the only fulcrum my life had rotated on. Now he has been replaced by this handsome stranger. This man who can hurt me with such impunity. I suddenly feel so very alone and scared. I sit down quietly in one corner of the room and start my prayers in a soft undertone.

"*Om Bhur Bhuva Swaha*[6]..."

Ramesh

I hear her low voice chanting her prayers and turn my back to her. Such an ugly woman! What did I ever see in her? The children are still asleep, and I hear her murmuring to them to wake up. In a minute she'll be standing next to the bed, with my *chai*[7] in her hand. I let myself dream of Sonia once more. Slightly plump but oh, so very nubile. I think of my hands brushing the underside of her breasts as I measure her for her first grown up blouse. Sixteen and ready to wear a sari. My mouth salivates at the thought of her exposed belly, at once round and luscious. Then I think of all the angular edges and concavity of my wife and sigh!

"Chai," she proffers softly, gazing down at me. I never look at her directly if I can help it. I can't stand to. I feel cheated every time I do. The dowry is long gone. The business it went into, long sunk. A bad omen if there ever was one! They say a woman brings luck and wealth to a man...she is the Goddess *Lakshmi* herself. Mine has brought nothing but ill luck and misfortune. I am still a poor tailor slogging all the hours God has given, while she, sits like a memsahib at home, taking care of the two brats. Pah! It was a sad day that I agreed to this alliance.

Sujata

He leaves for work, dropping the children off to school on the way. I wait a half hour, then quickly change into my work clothes. The new mistress is strict and doesn't like late comers. I have three houses now, and I find them hard to juggle. But it's necessary to keep it a secret from him. His pride would be injured if he knew I was working as a cleaner. After all, as the man of the house, he wants to be the provider. I can understand this.

Yet, the money he brings in is not enough. It barely pays the rent on this two-room tenement. I still have the school fees and all the expenses to take care of. My salary relieves him of the burden of it all. Oh, but he mustn't know!

The children come home at 2pm. After a quick lunch, I sit them down to study. I watch their heads bent over their books with a silent pride. They will be educated. They will have all the opportunities that I didn't. They will have the freedom denied to me.

He comes home late, swaying and slurring. I tug his shoes off and tuck him into bed.

"Sonia...," he whispers, grabbing me. I gently remove his arm and pull the sheet over him.

Ramesh

"You rotten, ungrateful wretch!" I scream at her. She is deaf to my anger and to my pleas. Her mother stands next to her, uncertain of her loyalty.

I turn and lash out at her. "This is all your fault! Encouraging her to study. No girl in our family has ever been to University. She should have been married by now. What is she going to do there? Have boyfriends? Sleep around? Give our family a bad name!" I raise my hand to strike her, and find my wrist seized by my son.

He towers over me but speaks quietly, "You will not hit *Maa*. Never again. Do you understand *Paa?* Never again."

I look into his eyes, so similar to mine, and feel a sudden fear.

When did they grow up so much? My daughter, so beautiful and so independent. My son, strong and ferocious in his defence of his mother.

I turn away defiantly. I will go to Rita. My little concubine who gives me the solace and the pleasure that I do not find in this vipers' nest.

Sujata

My daughter, the lawyer! The tears fall of their own volition. It's as though a dam has broken, and I cannot stop. They hug me on either side and urge me to stop crying. They don't understand. These are tears of joy!

Her cases are packed, and she is leaving for Delhi tomorrow. I wonder why I feel as though a part of me is being amputated. This is what I have worked towards. I shake my head at my folly and try and phone their father. He has been spending increasing amounts of time with that wretched Rita.

She answers, simpering into the receiver. I can hear his voice in the background. He refuses to come to the phone.

My son gently replaces the phone into its cradle. He hugs me and says, "It's okay, *Maa*. I'm still here. Don't worry. I'll take care of you."

I let myself lean against him, face awash with tears once more.

. . .

Ramesh

It is a grand house he lives in, my son. I feel my chest swell with pride. **My son!** Surely, he won't begrudge me a few thousand rupees.

He keeps me waiting for over an hour. My pride is rapidly replaced with a slow burning anger. How dare he? I am his father!

Yet, when he walks in, all smart in his dark blue suit, I stand up unbidden.

"Yes?" He queries curtly.

"For your mother's medicines…" I explain haltingly.

He raises an eyebrow at this and quickly makes out a cheque. I grab it and try to thank him.

"Don't bother, *Paa*. And don't lie either. Take it and drink yourself into the grave. Give *Maa* my love and tell her from me that I cannot understand how she insists on staying with a monster like you."

I back out hastily and make my way to the nearest bar.

Sujata

They have come to take me with them, once again. My daughter. My son. Their beautiful families. I smile at them weakly from the bed and nod my dissent once more. I am so happy to see them all. So happy to see them prosperous and content. A single tear rolls out of the corner of my eye inconspicuously. But my place is with my husband. The man I was pledged to, all those years ago. Mr. Ramesh Singh Ghaturia. I smile again at the memories that at once seem so vivid and so distant. I close my eyes. It is time to rest.

Ramesh

She is dressed in that same fuchsia sari from the wedding. They have put a big vermillion dot on her forehead. She looks so calm; so peaceful. The priests are chanting,

"*Ram Naam Satya Hai.*[8]"

We are carrying her to the pyre. I have to light the torch and set her aflame. All at once, our entire life together flashes before my eyes.

All at once, I see what she was for me: a rock that I took for granted, kicked and abused.

The priest urges me to light the pyre. I start to shake. I cannot do it. I cannot.

I throw myself on her lifeless body and sob. She's gone. My wife. My everything. They try and wrench me off her, but I won't let go. I look down at her face, and for the first and the last time, see the beauty in it.

Something inside me shrivels up and dies.

11
____

PALINDROME

DO you know what a palindrome is? It is a word, phrase or sequence that reads the same backwards as well as forwards.

My name is a palindrome. It wasn't meant to be, but it became one. Nayantara Deshpande is not a glamorous name, not for a film star. So, it was shortened to Nayan. Numerological calculations made by the studio's in-house priest deemed that no addition of a's or n's were required. So, unlike Teena, Saritaa, Prerrna, all debutantes launched alongside me, who had to endure the reconstruction of their names and live with it as long as their short-lived careers thrived, I got to retain my own name. How lucky was I!

So Nayantara Deshpande became Nayan, the ingenue being introduced by the great film maker Mohan Kumar. At fifteen, getting a break with Mohan Kumar was nothing short of a miracle. There were vicious rumours that my mother had slept with him to get me the role. Even more vicious were the ones that implied that I had. None true. Fact of the matter was that Mr. Mohan Kumar was gay. A closet homosexual who deliberately paraded as a ladies' man to keep the rumour mill churning.

"Nayan," he said to me before my screen test, "in this business, prepare to lose both your education and your reputation."

He was right, of course. I lost out on academic qualifications and my reputation was all but shredded, but what I gained in terms of knowledge, I would never have acquired out of books. Life, you see, is the greatest teacher of all.

THEY NICKNAMED ME 'THE WATER BABY'. My introductory shot was under a waterfall. The sari was a shade of nude that once wet, left very little to the imagination. Precisely the effect Mohan Kumar was going for. The censors cried foul but there wasn't much they could do, as technically I was clothed and taking a shower under a waterfall was what village belles did in most of our movies.

Of course, the irony of my nickname did not escape *Aai*[1]. I was born in the water after all.

"Why do you want to know the story again, *mulgee*[2]?"

"Because."

"Oh, very well..."

As *Aai* would launch into the story for the nth time, my imagination would take flight. Each time I would embellish the vivid pictures in my mind with further detail. It was as though I was there, in that village, walking down to the river with my *Aai*, heavily pregnant. As though, I could smell each blade of grass and the wet earth beneath it. The slight breeze that blew would caress my cheeks and ruffle my hair.

The morning sun would shine kindly upon the group of colourfully clad women who were taking their washing down to the river. One would hold *Aai*'s hand while the others teased her on her girth. They would sit her on the river bank and get started on unwrapping the clothes out of their different bundles. Some of them would hum, others would joke and laugh and trade stories of their husbands. *Aai* would join in time and again, happy to be away from the city, happy to be amidst her sisters, her friends, her family. Happy to put her feet up for a change. Then the pain would kick in and she would double over, gasping. They would pull her towards the river while one woman ran towards the village to get help.

Then she would bear down, pushing, screaming, crying while they would hold her arms, her head, her legs and speak to her in an ancient language. A language that all women shared from the beginning of Nature and of birth. I would come out glistening, rushing out into that river like a shooting star.

"You were smiling, they said, when you first came out. Like you already knew that you would conquer the world."

"I knew?"

"Yes, *mulgee*, you knew."

AS DESTINATION WEDDINGS GO, it isn't the most expensive or lavish one I've been to. Yet all this excess disgusts me. What a waste! Food that no one eats, outfits that are worn once and discarded, jewellery that's put away in bank lockers, what is the point of it all? All this money could feed a small village in India.

"You can take the girl out of the village…" Anand mocks me.

"Yes, yes, I know. But surely, Anand, you see where I'm coming from?"

"Nayan darling, it's been many years since you starved, eh?" He winks at me. Ah! Another dig at my weight.

I look at myself in the mirror and wonder why I let him taunt and demean me. If I challenge him, he'll say he is joking. If I ignore him, he'll say I'm sulking. So I paste a smile on my face and say, "You could do with losing a few kilos yourself, sweetie."

Then I walk out, a plastic smile on my plastic face to felicitate the bride and groom, and try my damnedest not to upstage them.

BABA WORKED as a peon in a small school in Virar, Mumbai. When he came to get *Aai* and his new born baby from the village, he was not

best pleased. A daughter was an encumbrance, a mouth to feed, a dowry to save up for. *Aai* tried to appease him.

"Look at her eyes, Nagesh. Everyone in the village said she has the most beautiful eyes they have ever seen on a baby. Look at those lashes....so long and thick. Isn't she the prettiest little thing? A star, our very own star. Let's call her Nayantara."

Baba had no interest in me or my name, not even in *Aai* after they returned to Mumbai. School in the day and being a foot soldier for a political party at night took up all his time. He did his duty towards us, but his interest lay elsewhere.

"Nagesh" *Aai* cribbed, "You are never home. We never get to see you or spend time with you. How is this a family?"

"Do you lack for anything? Have I not given you everything for yourself and the child? Think beyond yourself. Our party is doing work at grassroots level. We are representing those that have no voice. We are championing the underdogs. This is good work, it is God's work. I take pride in being a '*sainik*[3]'."

Then Baba would leave, returning at two, sometimes three in the morning.

At five, I was enrolled in the same school that Baba worked in. I was not allowed to acknowledge him as my father, but I would sneak looks at him each time he walked past, and on the rare occasions when he intercepted my look, he would frown or smile, depending on his mood.

I was not a particularly good student, nor was I a bad one. I was just an indifferent one. Studies left me cold. I understood that everyone needed to study to get ahead in life, but for me, those six hours were more about 'Baba spotting' than anything else. Regardless, I was a popular girl. My amiable personality and dimpled smile endeared me to the teachers. My mimicry skills and cutting sense of humour to my fellow students. I sailed through the first years of school purely on charm and charisma.

All that changed when Baba died.

∾

I HAVE the experience of a lifetime to know that I have looked for a father figure my entire life. From Mohan Kumar to all my lovers, ex-husbands and my current husband, I have searched for that elusive love, safety and comfort that only a father can give to his daughter.

I am dancing now in a safe and non-threatening way, swaying from side to side to the music, a Coca Cola Zero in my hand. I know there are all sorts of lenses trained on me and videos of me partaking in the festivities will soon be on all the news channels, in magazines and newspapers. I wonder what they'd say if I broke into gyrations now? Rubbed up against the men like I used to in my earlier films? Would they call me a 'sexy siren', a 'nubile nymphet' or would I be labelled a crass, over-the-hill diva trying to recapture her youth? The thought makes me giggle inadvertently. My sister-in-law, all heavy gold jewellery and lipstick that bleeds from the corners of her mouth, stares at me questioningly. I shake my head at her. All good.

"I need to get some food, Shobha."

"We can order a salad from room service later, Nayan."

I nod and swallow my disappointment. I was looking forward to the buffet. My first real meal in so many months. No wonder Anand has planted his sister next to me! She's the watchdog... a watchbitch? I cough to mask another giggle. This, without even the sneaky drink I have every night. What is wrong with me?

THE MAN who stood at the door was just another foot soldier picked for his ability to look sympathetic and aloof at the same time. His demeanour suggested that although he was extremely sorry to impart the news of Baba's death to us, there was not much else he could or would do, in terms of providing us with any monetary aid or emotional support.

"His work was completely voluntary, of course. No salary. He wanted to help people, you see."

"What about us? Where will we go now? What will we do? He was the sole earning member of this family..."

My mother was crying and choking on her words, and perhaps some of that penetrated his armour.

"You could come by the headquarters after the cremation. Maybe Dada, our party leader, can find you some work? Bring the child with you."

So *Aai* and I trooped over to Mahim leaving Baba's pyre still burning. We had been the only two people at the cremation. No other 'sainiks' had turned up to show their support. They must have been busy doing good elsewhere.

Children love their parents unconditionally, and just as an ugly child is still beautiful to its mother, a mother is always beautiful to a child. My *Aai*, however, was truly a beautiful woman. Something that did not go unnoticed by Dada.

He chewed *paan* [4] as he appraised us, spitting coloured saliva into the spittoon a lackey held to his side. His bulbous eyes took in her curves, lingered on her waist and alighted on her mouth. He barely glanced at me. A few drops of the betel juice had splattered on the sleeve of his white *kurta* [5] and I examined the pattern of the orange dots, fascinated. It looked like he had crushed a butterfly with his arm.

"I can see you need help, being a widow with such a young child. Normally, we don't employ women in our office here, but all my men are tired of the food the *dabbawallas* [6] bring. I can hire you as a cook. You would have to come in the evening, cook fresh food for everyone and leave after you've done the dishes. You can bring the child with you if you like."

"I am very grateful Dada" *Aai* kept her hands folded in front of her. "May I please return to my village first to fulfil all the rituals?"

Dada's phone had started ringing and he nodded his assent quickly, dismissing us with a wave of his hand.

THE GROOM LURCHES TOWARDS ME. It's obvious he's a little worse for the wear and I grab his arms as he nearly trips. He takes that as an invitation to launch into a close dance. His bride eyes him nervously from the podium.

"You are sssoo bbbeauttiful..." he slurs, practically slobbering over my cleavage. I'm also old enough to be his mother and am his bride's aunt through marriage. But I have enough experience of drunk men to know how to handle him.

I humour him for a while, slowly moving us towards his glowering father-in-law. With a raised eyebrow I indicate that I need ridding of this nuisance. As his arms are disengaged from my torso, he fires a parting salvo.

"Nandini...not a patch on you...No *namak*[7]!"

No *namak*. I always knew that. Nandini, my twenty-year-old daughter, just about to appear in her first film, is yet to find out.

Namak is the saltiness that a woman needs to be alluring and seductive. It's not enough to just be beautiful or talented or dance like a dream. *Namak* is that elusive but ineluctable seasoning that flavours every move, every flutter of the lashes, every slow smile. *Namak* promises the world but delivers just slivers of happiness. Celluloid wet dreams are made of this.

MY EVENINGS BECAME ABOUT CHOPPING vegetables and assisting *Aai* in the kitchen. I was an adept helper at the age of eight, and *Aai* would often hug me to her and whisper what a good little girl I was.

It had been a difficult homecoming for *Aai*. In returning to her village, maybe a part of her had hoped that she would be allowed to stay. Yet, her family was unwilling to saddle themselves with another two hungry mouths. It was made clear to her that we were no longer their responsibility. A fact that *Aai* had always known subconsciously. After all, it was drummed into all Indian girls that they were '*paraya dhan*': someone else's wealth. If that someone else was a man who had inconveniently dropped dead in his thirties and had no extended family or known assets, well, that was just too bad.

Aai was a proficient cook, but her food was not exactly finger licking good. It was edible and perhaps marginally better than the *dabbawallas'* fare. So, the men did not complain, and we managed to scrape a living out of it.

Travelling back on the train at night, I would often fall asleep in her lap. She would sing me songs from the movies to lull me to sleep. The rocking motion of the train along with her soft voice and her fingers running through my hair would live forever in my mind as the definition of pure, unadulterated love.

"MAMA, I'M BORED." Nandini has marched up to me and is pouting in that pretty way that always gets her what she wants.

"Darling, it's only for another hour or so. Go sit with your cousins for a while longer."

"All they're doing is taking selfies and posting them on Instagram. Can't I go back to the room?"

I look at my pouting, pretty child and sigh inwardly. Ours has not been the easiest relationship. I'd never wanted her and maybe that conveyed itself to her in the many ways that I remained disconnected. She was brought up by ayahs and although I underwrote every cost, she and I have remained planets that orbit at a safe distance from each other.

"What are you going to do in your room?"

"I'll read or watch a movie. I really can't be bothered to stay here any longer."

"Okay then, go. But do it discreetly or the family will be offended. If anyone asks, I'll say you had a headache."

"Thanks Mama, you're the best!" She blows me a perfunctory kiss and waltzes away.

Ah, I so wish I was.

INNOCENCE IS AN ARMOUR IN ITSELF. It took me seven years to realise that *Aai* was Dada's mistress. When I did, I had the most humongous meltdown.

"How could you cheapen yourself this way? What would Baba think? What must people think of us?"

She sat in front of me, chopping onions as I railed and cried and screamed. When I finally calmed down, she looked up and said, "I did what I had to do to survive."

I never questioned her after that. Survival, I learned, was a game with no rules.

THE PARTY IS WINDING down and most of the guests have departed. I had to sign quite a few autographs and I hope most of them don't end up on ebay or some other silly site. My signature is worth quite a lot, even now, even after all these years.

"Are the rumours true?" The producer's wife asks me.

"What rumours?"

"Of your comeback, of course. We've all been hearing about them. Besides, you're looking very svelte these days. The watermelon diet? And have you had some work done?"

I smile sweetly at her while what I really want to do is scratch her eyes out. None of your business, I want to scream. But one must adhere to the unwritten code of the industry. Always be nice. You never know who might come in handy one day.

"I've just come back from vacation Shyama. That's probably why I look so relaxed."

She knows I'm lying. We never speak openly about the 'work' we've had done. Our surgeons' names are more closely guarded than our bank accounts.

"Well, you'd better wait till after Nandini's debut, or they'll say you're in competition with your own daughter!" She laughs, revealing her yellowed teeth. I turn away.

My phone beeps and I excuse myself and go into the ladies' room.

The email has arrived. It confirms my suspicions. Anand has all but bankrupted me. His magnum opus was a colossal flop and as a co-producer, most of my money has evaporated along with his. Now, my comeback is not a vague possibility but an inevitability. The golden goose must learn to lay the golden eggs once again.

MOHAN KUMAR HAD COME to Dada's office one evening to complain about the studio boys who were playing up. They had unionised themselves and were asking for all kinds of perks.

"Dada, they'll ruin me at this rate. I'll never be able to get my movie off the ground…"

"What do you want me to do about it Mr. Kumar?"

"If one of your 'sainiks' could have a word with the union leader…"

Their negotiations had carried on for quite a while. Mohan Kumar had pledged a large sum of money to Dada and been assured of the party's support. Somewhere between their discussions and dinner being served, I had been spotted.

Aai had been reluctant at first. I was too young, too naive, too ill educated. Mohan Kumar had assured her that none of these would be obstacles. I had a *quality*, he had said, one he could spot a mile off.

Out of all the men that used and abused me in the film industry, perhaps Mohan Kumar was the kindest. My body had been a tool he had utilised to draw in the crowds, but he had treated me with a tenderness that wasn't always deserved.

When, puffed up with my own sense of importance and three movies in, I'd thrown a diva size tantrum, he'd taken me aside and given me a dressing down I'd never forget.

"Nayan, don't lose your head over success. Something that comes this easy can go just as easily. If you treat everyone you encounter on your way up kindly, they'll remember you on your way down too. The pages of this industry's history are littered with too many Johnny-come-latelys who thought they were indispensable. Who remembers them now? If you want a career, a long lived one, then stay humble, keep learning your craft and don't be afraid to try new things..."

Mohan Kumar died a few years later of AIDS. He never saw me reach the dizzying heights of success he'd predicted for me.

I REALLY NEED A DRINK. I go into the hotel bar where a few stragglers still remain. The barman recognises me immediately.

"Nayan madam, what can I get you?" He is a mixture of obsequiousness and glee and it repulses me. It takes every ounce of will power I have to give him a broad smile.

"A double scotch on the rocks."

His eyes widen at my choice but he pours an extra-large measure into the glass. I take it and retreat to a shadowy corner.

Is this what my life has come to? Drinking on the sly, on the verge of bankruptcy, on my fourth husband, with a daughter who couldn't care less if I lived or died? I feel a hundred years old, but my face is an unlined mask that I barely recognise. My spark was extinguished long ago and now I carry on because this is the only life I know.

One of my ex-husbands had been a keen amateur astronomer. Sometimes we'd lie together and look at the stars in the night sky. He would tell me about the various constellations. He'd talk about Ursa Major and Ursa Minor and try and trace their patterns out for me. I would pretend to follow, but rarely pay attention. The only thing I remember being struck by was the fact that some of those twinkling stars we were looking at had probably died thousands of years ago.

AAI HAD NOT GONE for Dada's cremation. Yet, she wore white every single day after his death. A widow's garb for a lover who never publicly acknowledged her existence. I suppose she must have loved him in her own way, as one learns to love the buoy that keeps one afloat.

I had gone to his memorial ceremony instead. I had worn white too, but my salwar kameez had been edged with Chantilly lace, and my lipstick had been a Chanel red. The sunglasses had been Dior and the bag had been Louis Vuitton. My head to toe designer look had been designed to scream excess, to announce my success in no uncertain terms.

My arrival at his memorial had signalled that I had indeed arrived. His wife and children's dirty looks had not daunted the shutterbugs. Click, click, click they'd gone. A bona fide superstar at the memorial. They had been unable to get enough of me. I had left everyone trailing in a haze of my perfume as I had bent down to touch the feet of his life size cutout.

I had known that from that moment on, his memorial would be about this picture and nothing else.

"Why did you hate him so much, *mulgee?*" *Aai* had asked, saddened by the show I'd put on.

"He used you *Aai*. You should have hated him too."

"Nayan, one day you will find that hate is too large a burden to carry."

"Come live with me *Aai*." I had never tired of requesting her nor her of refusing me.

"Your fancy living does not suit me, child. I am happy here. You have provided me with more than enough."

Two months later, *Aai* had passed away quietly in her sleep. Her body was not found for over a week. I had been on an overseas shoot, too busy breaking up my co-star's marriage.

FOUR WHISKEYS later I stagger back to my room. Anand is watching the television with the sound on mute. As soon as he hears me enter, he turns, furious.

"Where the hell have you been, Nayan?"

"In the bar, getting drunk."

"Are you in one of your moods again? Will I have to sit through the sob story of your life once more, you poor little rich girl?"

I start laughing.

"Poor or rich? Which one is it Anand?"

He observes me, puzzled.

"You need to sober up."

He strips me and then marches me towards the bathroom.

"Get in."

I climb meekly into the bath. He starts to fill it with lukewarm water. He leaves the taps running.

"We'll talk when you come out, okay?"

I close my eyes and let my body relax. The water pools and eddies around my body. I open my eyes and look down at my legs. How much thinner they are. They used to make fun of my 'thunder thighs' till I had the liposuction. My glance moves up to my slightly rounded stomach which has the trace of a caesarean scar. I touch it lightly. One unwanted pregnancy. The scars of the abortions are too well hidden. I look at my breasts and remember all the various hands that have fondled them, some rough and others gentle. I touch one nipple and feel it pucker immediately. I never offered this to my hungry baby, but other mouths latched on and sucked at it.

The water starts to overflow and I reach over to shut the taps. My hair swans around my head and I feel like a mermaid. A very drunk mermaid. I wiggle my toes and watch the ripples go through the water.

I submerge my body completely in the bathwater. I watch the bubbles rise to the surface. I watch the strange distortion of the ceiling from beneath the water and listen to the dub dub dub of my heartbeat.

My life has been a series of patterns. Some were open-ended, leading me somewhere and abandoning me there. Others were like closed loops, bringing me back to where I began. Some patterns have intersected with others, while others have diverged and taken me to solitary destinations.

Nayan nee Nayantara Deshpande's life has become a facsimile of her name. It has become a palindrome. I was born poor, I am poor again. I was born hungry, I am hungry again. I was born smiling, I am smiling again.

The water gurgles in my ears. My chest is expanding, desperate for air. Yet I refuse to break the surface.

Palindrome.

I was born in the water. It's only fitting that I die in it too.

DEAR ANIL

Dear Anil,

What was I before you? Did I exist? Was I relevant? Can I say this without betraying my feminist core?

You have been the one constant in my life, as long as I can remember. From the time that we were forced to sit next to each other in Year 3, and you engraved that line on the desk with your geometric compass, clearly demarcating your side from mine, you crept into my mind. I was terrified at first and then entranced.

You barely spoke to me the first two months. I was just a lowly girl and you were the smartest boy in the class. Even back then, you were so assured of your intellect that no one, not even the teachers, could win an argument against you. I think that may have been when I first fell a little in love with you.

Neither of us were remarkable looking. You, with your glasses and your slight hunch. Me, with my dark skin and plain features. No one would ever cast us as Romeo and Juliet in a school play. And yet, unbeknownst to you, I became your Juliet slowly, quietly.

In time you thawed. I was the only girl you that you allowed into your personal space. We shared lunches and sometimes, confidences. Your other friends looked upon me with suspicion. Who was this girl usurping their place? I said nothing, but I stayed by your side, fore-going female friendships in favour of you. Only you.

A few years later you told me of your dreams to go to the Indian Institute of Technology. You wanted to study engineering. You wanted to change the world with your inventions. I told you of mine; to be a writer. To write a book like 'Gone with the Wind'. You countered that I hadn't lived through a civil war. But that wasn't the point, I wanted to cry. I listened to you intently. You half listened. My dreams seemed so frivolous compared to yours.

In Year 8, we were separated. You chose to study Sanskrit, that archaic, opaque language. I chose French. That was the first time we argued. You said I was bailing out of a tough course and I said you were stuck in the past. Our friends called it a lovers tiff.

Years went by. We still sat together at lunch time and we still phoned each other after school. We still confided our hopes, our dreams, our petty grievances and our daily worries in each other. My parents asked if you were my boyfriend. You claimed that I was the sister you never had. I said nothing.

At our Leavers' do, you held my hand as I wept softly into my handkerchief. Leaving school was the scariest feeling in the world, and I was an emotional mess listening to all the speeches. You were unmoved by it all and elated at the thought of finally making your mark in the world. You didn't understand my sorrow, but you were kind enough not to mock me for it.

We went our separate ways. You pursued your dream and joined the IIT. I started my undergrad degree in English Honours. You discovered booze and cigarettes. I discovered Chaucer and Milton. We still spoke every week and met up every Sunday, but life was starting to pull us apart.

I still remember when you confided in me about your first crush. Girls had been unknown territory to you up until then. Yet, what a spectacular crush that was! A professor's daughter, hazel eyed and slim hipped, with hair she wore long and loose, and a smile she used to tease and tantalise all the boys who were madly in love with her. You wouldn't stop talking about her, and it crushed me.

You smartened yourself up. Hair gels and colognes entered your lexicon. Shirts became more fashionable and jeans tighter. When she finally and inevitably dashed your hopes, you refused to return to your slovenly ways. You liked the 'new you', and you were planning to take this 'new you' places.

You would tease me about my *jhola*[1] carrying ways. With my *salwar kameezes*[2] and *jooda*[3], I looked like a *behenji*[4] you would say. It hurt more than I let show. Since when had appearances become so important to you?

Papa got transferred to Chennai, and I chose to leave with the family rather than stay in Delhi. You called me a coward and said I was unable to sever the umbilical cord. That, at twenty, I should be independent and learn to navigate life on my own. You never once asked me nicely to stay or I might have done.

With distance, the chasm between us widened. I would still hear from you sporadically, but the emails were always rushed with little detail in them. I knew you were studying hard and were focussed on moving to the US. My course work had increased as well, and a new city brought new challenges into my life.

Sometimes I would wonder if you missed me. I missed you desperately, but by then it was crystal clear that I was no more than a friend to you. You were so much more to me.

Time has a funny way of lessening the pain, if not altogether deadening it. My sister's marriage, my Master's degree, my father's retirement, my mother's ill health started occupying enough head space for me to relegate you to a corner of my mind.

Once in a while, I'd pull out the file of our memories from the recesses of my mind, dust it off and examine it afresh. There was a bittersweet poignancy to knowing that I would never love anyone as much as I loved you. Yet, you could never be mine.

In time you left for the United States of America. To San Francisco, the city of golden bridges and gilt-edged dreams. I got hired by a local newspaper. Now, the only news I ever got of you was from school friends who passed through Chennai. They would look at me with barely disguised pity. Some would broach the subject of our past trying to ascertain what went wrong. I would laugh it off and change the topic. What was there to say?

The news of your marriage rocked my world. It was an email you had deigned to send me after nearly a year of no news. Her name was Amanda, Mandy for short. She was young, beautiful, eloquent and athletic. Your perfect woman. You were deliriously in love. Your parents approved, and could I come to the wedding as well?

I laughed through my tears. My pittance of a salary could barely afford me a visa let alone a ticket to your golden shores. I sent my congratulations in a card, and then stumbled into an affair with a colleague.

I lost my virginity to him in a dingy flat, eyes closed, imagining it was you. It was a tedious business, this love affair that involved no love. I was in it to forget you. He was in it for the sex. We limped along for nearly two years, and in my mind, I imagined your perfect life with your perfect wife and turned bitter.

I was the mistress of running away as you had always said. So, when the opening in the Bengaluru office came up, I didn't look back. I needed to get away from everything and everyone, most especially anyone who reminded me of you.

It was nearly three years later that I heard of your divorce. You'd discovered your perfect Mandy *in flagrante delicto* with an ex-flame. I shouldn't have, nevertheless I guiltily savoured the news. Never once did I question why this tidbit had come to me second hand. Perhaps the hope that I might stand a chance now blinded me to the obvious fact that I was no longer very significant in your life. Not significant enough for you to inform me of your change in circumstance yourself.

I wrote to you and waited in vain for a response. When none came, even that slight hope extinguished itself.

Life might have carried on with us never crossing each other's paths. For the next ten years it did. I strayed in and out of relationships, lost my mother to cancer, saw my father's disappointment in my refusal to settle down, saw my sister's envy of my career and independence, and despite everything, felt at peace with myself.

Had I not run into you in that book shop in Delhi, how differently things would have turned out. We met as old friends meet; reticent at first, observing the differences time had wrought on our appearance. The grey hair, the wrinkles, the extra weight. Then quickly moving past the superficial to the nub of the matter. Did we still like one another?

Over coffee we discovered that yes, we still did. I asked you why you never responded to my letter and you countered that you had never received it. Mandy had been spiteful enough to withhold all correspondence from you. She had been vicious enough 'to take you for every last dime'. I noticed the dejection in your voice and the defeat in your shoulders. My heart went out to you.

I was in Delhi for a week for work and we met nearly every day. Quick coffees, wines chugged hurriedly, rushed dinners and so many laughs. I'd forgotten how funny you were. How we made each other laugh.

On my last night in Delhi I called you up to my hotel room. I knew what I wanted but I wasn't sure that you did. Had enough time passed for you to view me as a woman and not as your substitute sister?

Our lovemaking was tentative and exploratory at first. Then it was fierce and passionate, exhausting and exhilarating. I clung to you afterwards unable to believe my luck. It was then that you broke it to me. You planned on going back to the US. *This* was a mistake. You were not ready for a relationship. We should have just stayed friends.

I don't remember the flight back to Bengaluru, nor the months that followed. I don't remember shedding any tears either. I just remember ignoring your calls, texts, letters, emails - all attempts to reach me. Till you finally stopped.

I wonder if you ever felt any guilt over that night? I had bared myself body and soul, and you had rejected me once again.

Mithun entered my life sometime around then. He was just a junior and I treated him as a flunkey for a very long time. He says he fell in love with me straight away, but it took him many months to work up the courage to ask me out. I was taken aback by his interest. I was too damaged by then and rebuffed him repeatedly.

His persistence wore me down eventually. I guess I found a kind of happiness with him. You called it a 'compromise' later. Maybe it was, but it was a heck of a lot more than you had ever given me.

He knew all about you. I wanted a fresh start, and I wanted to purge myself of you before I gave whatever remained to Mithun. He was kind and compassionate, and so in love with me. I tried. I really, really tried. But he wasn't you.

Your father's Alzheimer's had called you back to India, and this time you chose not to contact me. As you took care of him, your mother introduced you to many suitable girls. At forty you still had traces of rebellion left in you, and the thought of an 'arranged marriage' repulsed you. She harangued you constantly, painting visions of a lonely old age, of dying undetected and unloved.

Rashmi, our common friend, told me all this over a pitcher of Sangria on a Sunday afternoon. Mithun had gone to the Men's room in the restaurant and she filled me in hurriedly, constantly looking over her shoulder. She asked me to get in touch and I refused point blank. I saw the hurt on her face, but I had closed the door on that chapter of my life. Nothing would make me reopen old wounds. Famous last words, huh?

I often wonder why neither of us had children. I could have, with Mithun. You must have thought about it with Mandy? I think we would have made good parents: involved, engaged and kind parents. Life denied us that chance as well.

You would probably say that you became a father when your father became a child. I saw firsthand how you looked after him. The love, the sensitivity, the patience you handled him with. It couldn't have been easy. You gave up all hopes of a successful career and became your parents' caretaker. You, who were meant to soar, to conquer, to vanquish.

I soared instead. From sub-editor I became editor. My pen was respected and feared. I was adamantine, incorruptible, ruthless. I took down crooked politicians and mercenary businessmen with impunity. All it took was a single editorial. I won awards, I was invited to sit on panels and International juries. Did you watch me soar? Did you miss me then?

Seven years after our ill-fated night together, I found myself dialling your number. You sounded weary but pleased to hear from me. I invited myself over. I watched as you fed your father and put him to bed. I observed the bald patch on your head, and the tremor in your hands. Your mother fussed over me, only seeing the aura of celebrity. It was you who took my hands in yours later and asked if I was happy.

How many hearts can be broken in a lifetime? No, let me rephrase that. How many times can one heart be broken in a lifetime?

Yours broke a second time when your father died. After Mandy, he was the only one who had held your heart in the palm of his hand. He had been your hero, your idol, your purpose, your everything. I broke Mithun's when I left him with no explanation, to be by your side.

We were in our fifties. It took us the better part of our lives to realise that we belonged together. How long did we have with each other? A year or two? Was it enough? Could it ever be enough?

Dear Anil, my very dearest Anil, towards the end you thanked me for giving you a sliver of happiness. I had wanted to give you a lifetime, my darling.

They are preparing your body for the Crematorium. Only the menfolk are allowed to bathe and dress you. But, before you are turned to smoke and ash and dust, I will put this letter upon your chest. This letter that contains the story of our sad, incomplete love. That chest on which I would lay my head sometimes and listen to the beat of your heart. That heart which finally broke into smithereens.

How will I carry on without you?

I cannot let you go. I <u>have</u> to let you go. What other possible end could our story have had?

All my love - forever,

Shonali.

13

UNREQUITED

I sense him before I see him. It's always been that way. I had forgotten the feeling. Except that now it revisits me. The goose-bumps that appear quite suddenly on my arms. The slight shiver that accompanies them. I scan the room quickly, trying to be as discreet as possible. My drinking buddies engrossed in their conversation and cocktails, barely notice. I spot him at once. He's at the bar. Alone.

I perch myself precariously next to him, leaning forward to catch the barman's eye, maximising my cleavage, to give him an eyeful.

Does he remember me?

He turns slightly, takes in the wares, smiles into his drink, and turns away. I pay the grinning barman quickly, and totter back to my table, thinking fast on my feet.

"Miss?" He calls out behind me. "You dropped your scarf."

I don't respond, ignoring him deliberately. As I sit myself down, he appears next to me.

"Your scarf?"

I look up and smile, registering surprise and gratitude.

"Why, thank you! I hadn't noticed. How kind of you. Please, do join us... Let me buy you a drink..."

He hesitates, then looks at me again, taking in the short dress that clings provocatively to my curves, the shapely leg that swings back and forth in invitation, and says, "Yes, okay. Why not?"

Does he remember me?

There are introductions, more cocktails, and then a colleague shouts out,

"Time for tequila shots! It's Deepika's birthday after all."

"It's your birthday?" He asks, focussing on me.

"Yes." I respond, searching his eyes for a spark of recognition.

"Then this round's on me."

THE LIFT IS CROWDED with late night revellers, smelling of stale cigarettes and too much alcohol. I press against him, my heart tattooing a wild beat inside of me. I can't remember if he asked me, or I suggested it. Coffee! What a euphemism for what is about to happen.

Inside his hotel room, he throws aside his jacket and grabs me in one move. His mouth is upon me, and my sigh gets buried deep inside my throat. His tongue pushes my lips apart, plunges into me, tasting, feeling, probing... I kiss him back with a desperate hunger. My fingers are ensnared in his hair and I pull him towards the bed. We fall upon it together, laughing, mad in our lust.

He tugs at my dress, pulling down the straps, exposing my ample breasts to his hot gaze. The dress bunches underneath, pushing the orbs up, offering them up to him, to do what he will. He licks a trail between them, his tongue sending ripples of desire coursing through me. Deliberately, maddeningly, he avoids my nipples, even as they pucker, waiting to be sucked, to be bitten, to be swallowed up whole. I moan and pull his head towards them. He laughs and pulls my dress down further. His fingers are at once strange and familiar. I lie there exposed, but for a sliver of cloth that covers the molten centre of me.

He leaves me there and quickly unzips his jeans, kicking them aside and begins to unbutton his shirt. His erection springs up: large, proudly tumescent, throbbing, a purple hue. I gaze up at him.

Does he remember me?

Skin upon skin. I feel like I'm burning up. He trails kisses down my stomach down to between my legs, where he pauses, and then blows ever so slightly, to part the curls that are dampened, awaiting his arrival. His tongue darts in, exploring me, tasting me. Wantonly I moan, my head thrashing side to side. Bolts of pleasure shoot through me, very nearly sending me over the edge. But he withdraws again. His mouth searches mine and I taste myself upon him. His taste, my taste and the tequila mingling into a cocktail that quenches a long-forgotten thirst.

"Vishal..." I whisper against his mouth.

"Hmmm?"

"I want you...now...please..."

He parts my legs with his knee, and enters me swiftly. I am ready to receive him, and I stretch to accommodate his widened girth. We fall into a rhythm almost immediately, his chest hair tickling my nipples into even tinier buds. I feel so full, so complete, so at home, that I find myself wrapping my legs around him, to pull him in even deeper. I try and look into his eyes, but they are closed, his face contorting in pleasure. He is so close, and I find myself upping the tempo, to keep up. He roars his arrival and my whimper of an orgasm is nearly drowned out. Spent, he falls upon me, and I almost cannot breathe, but don't want him to move. To remove his weight off me, to remove himself from inside me.

We lie wrapped up together for a while, his sweat, a damp, musky smell that merges with the unmistakable scent of sex. Thrilling, fulfilling sex.

Does he remember me?

We make love again, changing positions. I straddle him. He spoons me. I take him in my mouth, and drink in every precious drop of him. We barely pause for breath. There is too much to explore. Desire ricochets off the walls of our room, and if anyone can hear our moans of pleasure, we are too beyond caring.

Night slides into morning, and we finally fall asleep, exhausted from our frenetic coupling. His hand cups my breast, and I feel his limp member press up against my bottom. I lie there, floating euphorically in a post coital glow.

"DEEPIKA?" He murmurs into my ear.

"Mmmm?" I ask sleepily.

"Dinner tonight?"

I smile languidly and stretch.

He goes in to shower. I can hear him singing.

His number is written on the notepad. I examine it. It's only taken ten years. Ten agonising years of being discounted, rejected, passed over.

Ten agonising years of wanting what I couldn't have. Ten agonising years of waiting, watching, hating myself for my weakness.

Ten years, and now I have him.

I smile and tear the paper into several pieces. The scraps scatter on to the carpet. I pick up my handbag and walk out without a backward glance.

14

THE STRINGS THAT BIND US

2 **007**

THE text arrived sometime in the morning. Ruchi opened it on the train on her commute to work. It simply said - She died last night and I am so, so sad today. No one will understand except you. Call me when you can. Tara. xx

Her heart clenched at the awful sadness of it all. Memories came flooding back. Memories of Summer holidays spent miles away from home. Memories of one particular holiday that could never ever be erased.

～

1985

"IS she your grandmother?" Ruchi asked.

"No, silly. Our grandmother lives in Dehradun."

"I know that! I meant, your other grandmother. Your Papa's mother."

"No, she's not. Now come on, it's your turn."

Ruchi looked out at the old lady sitting alone on the verandah and wondered why Tara wouldn't talk about her. What was the big secret?

She looked down at the Snakes and Ladders board game and realised that she was losing. The old lady was soon forgotten in her hasty attempts to catch up to Tara.

It had been three years since she'd last visited Delhi. She'd forgotten how hot it could get in the Summer. Mummy had said it was best if they gave the British Summer a miss this year. After all, it had rained continuously the previous couple of years, and a bit of heat was what they both needed. Didn't Daddy need or want the heat as well? Mummy had slammed the case shut and said Daddy's needs were not her priority any more.

THEY LAY TOGETHER on the bed, lazily skimming through Tara's well-thumbed Archie comics.

"Don't you read anything else?"

"I do too! I read *Chacha Chaudhry*[1] and *Amar Chitra Katha*.[2]"

"Those are all comics. I meant books - proper books."

"What for? Books don't have pictures in them. I like comics. They are colourful and they make me happy."

Once again, Ruchi pondered the differences between her cousin-sister and herself. Considering their mothers were twins and they themselves were only eight months apart, Tara and she had so little in common.

Admittedly they lived on two different continents, spoke only occasionally on expensive international phone calls and met sporadically every few years, but surely genetically they should have been more similar than they were?

Tara was shorter than her and squatter too, but she had a prettier face. Ruchi often wondered why she hadn't inherited her mother's lovely, delicate features and instead had her father's broad nose, high forehead and fuller lips. Temperamentally as well, they were like chalk and cheese. Tara was impetuous, demanding, sporty and street smart while Ruchi was shy, a bookworm that preferred day dreaming to any kind of physical exertion.

"Ever flown a kite?" Tara asked suddenly.

"No…"

Ruchi was wary of Tara's light bulb moments. It invariably landed them in trouble. Like the time she had insisted on climbing the water tank on the second floor of the neighbour's building, nearly killing them in the process. Or when she had taken the scissors to Ruchi's hair in an attempt to copy Zeenat Aman, the film heroine's hairstyle. Ruchi had had to live with a lopsided fringe till her mother relented to letting it be cut professionally. Somehow, blessed as she was with the gift of the gab, Tara always managed to escape punishment.

"Let's do it this evening. I'll get Ramu to get us some kites and we can fly them. What's your favourite colour?"

"Uhhh, orange?"

"Orange? Yuck! I prefer magenta. But that's okay. They'll look pretty flying side by side."

Tara had a way with words and soon Ruchi found herself visualising the kites bobbing and dipping alongside each other, against a bright blue sky.

WHAT TARA HAD NEGLECTED to mention was that she had no money to buy these kites. Ramu, their seventeen-year-old servant boy, stood sullenly refusing to let Tara *didi* [3]borrow the money out of his wages.

"Ramu *bhaiyya*[4], I will give it back, I promise!"

Another adamant shake of his head. His wages were sent to his family in Nepal. He lived in the little *barsati* [5]room and ate all his meals with the family. His clothes were all hand-me-downs from Tara's papa. The few rupees he had were spent on the sneaky *beedis*[6] he smoked, and he was loath to give it to a pair of ten year old girls for their silly, fanciful ideas. There was no budging him and Tara had to concede defeat.

"There has to be a way…" Tara whispered at lunch time. Ruchi kept pushing the *bhindi*[7] around on her plate. Okra was her least favourite vegetable and her immediate concern was how to camou-flage the fact that she had no intention of eating the slimy mess she had created.

"Tara!" *Mausi* [8]glared at her daughter. "How many times have I told you, no chatting at meal times."

"Sorry Mumma."

Tara wasn't sorry in the least, Ruchi could tell. Her brow was furrowed in a familiar way. She was plotting something, and this worried her. No good ever came out of Tara's plots.

"Has he called?" *Mausi* asked Mummy.

"No, and I don't think he will."

"Maybe you should…?"

"Chetna, I'm done! It's always me making amends, apologising, being a sap. Enough is enough."

"Chitra, have you thought of the alternative? Really thought it through?"

"I have…but let's talk about it later. Big ears around. Ruchi, eat your *bhindi*!"

IN *MAUSI'S* TWO-STOREY HOUSE, the main residents lived downstairs. There was *Mausi, Mausa*[9] (Amit), Tara and her two-year-old brother Tarun. Ruchi and her mother occupied the fourth bedroom temporarily as their house guests. When they left, it would go back to being a storage room for all their winter duvets, coats and assorted paraphernalia.

Upstairs, on the roof, were two and a half *barsati* [10]rooms plus a common bathroom and a huge verandah. One room was occupied by Ramu, the other by the mysterious old woman, and the tiny little room housed the *Mandir*[11].

All good Hindu households had a little *Mandir*, a shrine for their pantheon of Gods and Goddesses. Whether this took the form of a little corner in a room, or whether, in the more prosperous house-holds, it had an entire room dedicated to it, a *Mandir* was part and parcel of a proper Hindu household. This *Mandir* would house multiple idols of various Gods, the prominent one (the God of the household) receiving pride of place in the centre.

Every morning, each person in *Mausi*'s household would congregate in the little *Mandir*. *Mausi* would light the *diya*[12], offer prayers and give everyone a bit of the fresh homemade *prasad*[13], after having presented it to the Gods. She would also put in some coins in a copper pot filled with oil as a thank you for keeping her family healthy, safe and affluent.

"I think there maybe enough change in there to buy our kites." Tara announced this with nonchalance.

"Steal from the Gods?!" Ruchi gasped at the temerity of her suggestion.

Although they were not particularly religious back home, she still carried a lot of reverence and superstition within her. Particularly as these rituals seemed so exotic, so remote and filled with such a strange beauty that her mundane life in London did not possess.

"We are not stealing, we are just borrowing. I will return the coins once I get my pocket money. The Gods won't mind. What are they going to do with the coins anyway?"

Tara's logic was irrefutable, and although Ruchi was older by eight months she was the more timid of the two, and always easily led.

STEALING the coins was not a problem, it was getting the oil off them. They wiped with all their might, but the coins remained greasy. So much so, that the kite seller looked very suspiciously at them as they procured two of his cheaper kites. Excited with their purchases they walked home in the balmy Summer evening.

"Do you actually know how to fly a kite, Tara?"

"No, but Ramu can show us. I'm sure he does. It can't be that difficult, can it?"

Once again Ramu was summoned to the terrace. This time, however, a childlike glee overtook him as he eyed their kites.

Yes, he nodded, only too happy to show the two inexperienced kite flyers how it was done.

It was breezy on the terrace and the old lady sat in her usual spot, looking down at the passersby on the street below. Her hands worked on the beads she held as she mouthed quiet prayers, or what they assumed were prayers. They'd never actually heard a word emerge from her. Ramu went up to her and said something. She looked at him, then nodded quickly. She picked up her little seat, the *mooda* [14]and moved it over to the side, so that they could have the run of the terrace. Her attention had now shifted from the street to Ramu and the girls.

Quickly and efficiently Ramu tied the strings to the kites. Then he explained in his broken Hindi that one of them would have to hold up the kite and let go at the exact moment that he indicated. Turning his face towards the peepul tree, he watched as the breeze ruffled the leaves, and then turned to Tara suddenly and yelled, "*Abhi*[15]!"

Tara let go of her magenta and green kite, and they watched as it climbed while Ramu yanked at the string in smooth movements. When the kite had ascended high enough, he called Tara over and handed her the string, explaining what she had to do to keep her kite up in the air.

It was Ruchi's turn next and she swallowed a lump in her throat, thrilled to bits but scared that she was unequal to the task. Ramu was a patient teacher, and no matter how many times her kite crash landed, he would resume his instructions seamlessly. Twenty minutes later she managed to get the hang of it and her kite was in the sky, alongside Tara's, swooping, dipping, flying, just as they had imagined.

Ramu stood by watching them with a sort of paternal pride. He really was a kind fellow despite his occasional grumpiness. The old lady watched the kites, her mouth still moving in prayer. The four made an odd quartet, but that evening there was an unusual sympathy between them. They were from different worlds but were united in that moment; a moment of pure, innocent, unalloyed joy.

$\cdot$ $\cdot$ $\cdot$

OF COURSE, it would end in tears. Even as they watched their kites fly high, other kites joined them. The sky above them was overrun by a riot of colours - blue, green, yellow, red, magenta and orange. Fluttering, soaring, diving, gliding, plunging.

Till one of them headed for Ruchi's kite. Ramu tried to help her. They yanked at the string together, trying to escape from the predatory green kite but it followed, swooping and circling, entangling her string with his, till he cut right through it. They heard a roar go up on the neighbouring terrace and two young boys ran towards the felled kite.

Ruchi barely had time to register her loss because the green kite was now heading towards Tara's.

"Ramu!!" Tara screamed. They tried pulling at the string wanting to bring the kite back down. The wind had picked up and the kite wouldn't descend, not as quickly as they wanted. The green kite made short work of Tara's string and before long, all they held in their hands were strings leading to nothing.

"Kaanch[16]." Ramu muttered. He indicated that the neighbourhood boys had lined their strings with crushed glass. All the quicker to cut an adversary's string and add the kite to their collection.

"Bullies!" cried Tara. She was inconsolable. All that plotting, planning and thieving for half an hour of pleasure.

Somewhere inside Ruchi she wondered if the Gods hadn't seen fit to punish them for their deeds.

"AMIT, I think Ramu is stealing from us." *Mausi* said sotto voce.

"What makes you think that Chetna?" *Mausa* frowned at his wife.

"Well, I was cleaning the *puja thaali* [17]and the copper pot felt strangely light. I emptied it out and a lot of the coins were missing."

Ruchi's mouth had fallen open at the dinner table. Tara kicked her under the table. Ruchi hastily composed her features.

"You can't trust these servants I tell you." Ruchi's mother entered the fray. "Remember Billu *kaka*[18] all those years ago Chetna? He stole all of Dad's expensive pens and sold them. At least I don't have to worry about thieving servants in London."

Ruchi gazed in horror at the elders. Where was this headed and what would they do to Ramu?

"Chetna, you don't keep count of the coins and there is no proof. We can't go around accusing Ramu without knowing for sure."

"Yes, but Amit, if he's stealing from the *puja* pot, how soon before he starts stealing from us? Maybe he already is, and we haven't noticed."

"We did it." The words escaped Ruchi before she could think. She clapped her hands over her mouth as if to retrieve the confession, but the damage was done.

Tara glared at her.

"Is this true Tara?" Amit *Mausa* looked at his daughter.

"Yes, papa."

"And when exactly were you planning to own up?"

AMIT *Mausa* rarely lost his temper, but when he did, woe betide anyone who was in the firing line. Tara and Ruchi found themselves squatting rooster style on the terrace, with their arms looped behind their knees, holding on to their ears like *murgas*[19]. The old woman watched silently from her *mooda.*

"Tara, my legs hurt." Ruchi whispered. She was unused to squatting and her mother's insistence at her partaking in the punishment had been unfair, she felt. If it weren't for her honesty, poor Ramu would have been facing some dire consequences.

"Too bad!" Tara whispered back. She still hadn't forgiven Ruchi. It's not like she hadn't planned to own up. She would have done it at a more opportune time, when her father wasn't around and the maximum punishment she would have received would have been a tight slap from her mother.

They squatted alongside each other in silence. From time to time, they would shift their weight, to get rid of the pins and needles in their legs. The old woman was cutting a *chikoo* fruit, and Ruchi yearned for a slice of the brown, deliciously sweet fruit.

Suddenly the old woman got up and came towards them. She smiled a toothless smile and gently inserted a piece of fruit each into their mouths. Astonished, they chewed in silence watching as she made her way back to her little seat.

"Who is she?" Ruchi asked Tara.

"I don't really know. We adopted her last year." Tara had forgotten her rancour.

The old woman kept feeding them the *chikoo* as they squatted and somehow, it made the pain and the embarrassment a bit more bearable.

"What do you mean - adopted?"

"I mean, one fine day I woke up and there she was. No one told me anything except that she was going to live with us. She helps with a few household chores, but mostly she just sits up here and watches the world go by."

"Is she related to you?"

"I don't think so. I'd never laid eyes on her before."

To Ruchi's mind, this was a mystery worth solving. Terrace climbing, temple thieving and kite flying may have been Tara's strengths, but like Sherlock Holmes, Ruchi much preferred using her mind.

A FONDNESS GREW between the girls and the woman. They would often take their board games and sit on the floor by her side. She would watch them silently, nodding and smiling, but never exchanging a word with them. Sometimes she'd reach forward and pat their heads, as though bestowing a quick blessing on them.

Ruchi tried asking Chetna. "Where is the old lady from, *Mausi*? Why do we call her *Biji*? Is she related to us? Why does she not speak? Is she mute?"

Mausi's answers were always vague or deliberately obtuse, and Ruchi felt they were hiding something from her. Her curiosity was piqued even more.

"Tara, don't you find it odd that no one tells us anything about the old lady?"

"Hmmmm?" Tara was busy polishing her toe nails with the nail varnish she'd sneaked out of her mother's wardrobe.

"I mean, who is she? Why is she living here? Where is her family? Why doesn't she speak?"

"Ruchi, you're too nosy. Who cares? If they wanted to tell us, they would have. And she is not mute. I heard her humming an old film song the other day."

Humming? This was news to her. Ruchi was determined to get more out of the old lady that evening. But first, there was the annoying business of the afternoon nap.

Every day after lunch, their mothers insisted that they nap for a couple of hours. The four of them would lie on *Mausi's* bed, the girls between the mothers. The cooler would be filled with water and the strange smell of dampened wood would fill the room. Then with a roar, the cooler would start, and cool air would emanate from between the slats of the monstrous machine. All of them, except Ruchi, found the sounds, the smells and the routine comforting. They would all fall asleep within minutes of each other, while she'd lie there, trying not to fidget, waiting for the purgatory of the afternoon nap to come to an end.

That afternoon as she lay there, her mind carving out strange day dreams, she heard her mother whisper to *Mausi*.

"Chetna, are you awake?"

"Mmmmm...just falling asleep Chitra. Can it wait?"

"I had a letter from Satish this morning."

"What? What did it say?"

"He's happy to let me start the divorce proceedings."

"So...you were right...there's always been someone else..."

"I told you things had changed after my last India visit. His behaviour, his attitude....It was like he had switched off from us. Like we were an inconvenience..."

Ruchi lay stock-still, her mind trying to process this information. Divorce? What did that mean? Would they have to come back to

India? Would she never see Daddy again? Would they live here with *Mausi*'s family? Would she go to a different school?

Tara groaned in her sleep suddenly and the conversation came to an abrupt end. She felt the change in the air but didn't dare open her eyes for fear her eavesdropping would be found out.

ALL THOUGHTS of the old lady's provenance were wiped clean from Ruchi's mind. More important matters occupied her now. The entire evening, she walked around in a daze, unable to comprehend how it had come to this. She had never heard her Mummy and Daddy arguing. They had never even exchanged a cross word in front of her. So, why were they divorcing?

"What's the matter with you?" Tara poked her in the ribs. "You've barely said a word all evening."

"Nothing."

"Then eat the samosa! If you don't want it, I'll have it."

Ruchi passed Tara her samosa. She had no appetite. They were sitting on the terrace, cross legged on the coir mat Ramu had rolled out for them. They had been given a samosa each with a small glass of Fanta orange as a treat. *Mausi* and Mummy were entertaining old friends downstairs and the goodies had been brought in to serve with tea.

"I wonder if those fat gossipy women will leave some *jalebi*[20] for us?" Tara said, licking the ketchup off her fingers.

The old lady laughed, and Ruchi looked up at her wonderingly. It was so easy to forget she was there. It would have been a perfect opening to ask her all the questions she wanted to, but today, her heart wasn't in it. Tara, on the other hand, decided to take up the mantle instead.

"*Biji*[21], who are you?"

The silence stretched out between them, indeterminately.

"I mean," Tara continued, with all the finesse of a bull in a china shop, "you're not family, so, why are you living with us?"

The old lady shook her head as though to clear it, then stood up, picked up her *mooda* and went into her room. She shut the door behind her.

Tara and Ruchi exchanged looks.

"I was just trying to find out for you...."

"You could have been nicer about it."

"I wasn't nasty!"

"You've upset her. What if she tells your parents?"

"Then let her. Not like I was doing anything wrong this time. Anyway, why are you so grumpy with me today?"

"I'm not."

"You are too! Is it to do with your Mummy and Daddy breaking up?"

"H...how do you know?"

"I knew long before you came. That's why you came here. So that *Mausi* could talk to us and to *Nani*[22] about what is to be done."

"SOMETIMES Ruchi, mummies and daddies stop getting along. Then, isn't it better that they go their separate ways rather than carry on living with each other and being unhappy?"

Ruchi nodded sadly between hiccups. She had cried for two hours straight and had been left with a swollen face and a penitent mother trying to explain her decision.

"W...why didn't you tell me?"

"Darling girl, I wanted to...but Mummy wasn't sure herself. I needed to talk to my mummy and my sister before I made the decision. I was going to tell you before we left for Dehradun."

"Is *Nani* angry with you?"

"No, not at all. She's just sad Ruchi. She wanted me to be happy with your daddy, but she understands that I'm not."

"Does this mean we will live with *Nani* now? Will I never get to see Daddy again?"

"Ruchi, sweetheart, of course you'll see Daddy again! There are so many things to be worked out, but I promise you, I will never keep you from seeing your father..."

They hugged and Ruchi thought that maybe divorce wasn't the worst thing in the world after all.

A MONTH later they returned from Dehradun to Delhi. Ruchi had spent that month reading as many books as she could get her hands on. *Nani*'s library was a treasure trove of classics and while she had immersed herself in Dickens and Austen, Mummy and *Nani* had spent hours talking.

It was a strange month filled with silences and sadness, but also with love, laughter and *Nani*'s famous carrot *halwa*[23]. Ruchi felt cocooned and protected, as though she was living in a bubble of books, gardens and maternal affection. *Nani* was a keen gardener and an avid reader. She was also a woman of silence. A retired lecturer, she had retreated from life and a lifetime of talking, to the hill station of her childhood. A self-imposed exile in which she thrived quietly amongst her plants and her books.

Mummy had called her into the living room one day while Nani sat in the armchair filling in her crossword puzzle.

"We will return to London, Ruchi. Mummy doesn't want to give up her job. Besides, your school and your friends are there, and it will be easier for you to see Daddy that way too. Are you happy with that?"

Ruchi had nodded quickly, catching Nani's glance towards Mummy. It had contained an inexplicable emotion, one that would take her years to decipher.

"SCHOOL IS SOOOOOO BORING RUCHI!" Tara moaned as she threw her satchel to one side. Ramu picked it up and put it on the chair.

"Tara didi, *Saraswati Maa*[24] will be angry! You must not throw your books on the floor."

Suitably admonished and fearful that the Goddess of learning would indeed smite her, Tara mouthed a quick sorry to him, then turned and grabbed Ruchi's hand, pulling her into the other room.

"I missed you! Why didn't you write?"

"I did. I just forgot to post them."

"Dumbo!" Tara laughed good naturedly. "I have so much to tell you. I found out more about *Biji*..."

"Really? What?"

All revelations had to wait till after lunch and their nap. Ruchi found herself falling into a dreamless sleep almost immediately, as though, in these two months her body had acclimatised to the routine like a native.

Later, as they climbed the stairs to the terrace, Ruchi realised that this was her last evening with Tara, and different as they were from one another, it wasn't just genes and family that bound them to each other, it was genuine affection. She quickly planted a kiss on Tara's cheek.

"Ewwww...what did you do that for?" Tara wiped her cheek, and immediately Ruchi felt annoyed with her again. There was a word for her cousin-sister... Insufferable. Tara was insufferable!

"*Biji*, look, Ruchi is back! Show her what you showed me." Tara jumped up and down excitedly in front of the old lady.

Biji looked up at Ruchi and smiled slowly. She tied the beads in her sari *pallu* and stood up unhurriedly. Then she shuffled off towards her room, beckoning the girls to follow.

Her room was basic with a small bed, an armoire and a tiny mirror on the wall. There was a little battered suitcase that sat beneath the bed, which she was pulling out. She unzipped the case and took out an envelope, which she handed to Tara.

Jubilantly, Tara pulled out a black and white photograph from the envelope.

"Look - this is *Biji* and her family."

In the photo, *Biji* sat on a chair flanked by a young man, an attractive young woman and their two daughters, who looked like they were roughly the same age as Tara and Ruchi.

"Your granddaughters?" Ruchi asked the old lady.

"Of course, silly!" Tara responded in her stead. "Why else do you think she likes us so much?"

"But where are they now? What happened to them?"

Tara pinched her hard.

"Owww!"

The old lady had started to weep quietly. She took the photo back from them, put it in the envelope and sat on her bed, tears rolling down her cheeks, her body shuddering.

Tara pulled her out of the room.

"You shouldn't have asked her that! She does that every time I ask."

"How was I to know?"

IN THE SPIRIT OF HONESTY, the girls confronted their mothers the same evening.

"Why don't you tell us more about *Biji*?"

"Who is she and where is her family?"

"We know she has a family. She showed us the photo."

"Why is she living here? Are they all dead?"

"Is she a ghost?"

This last one was Ruchi's invention, and three pairs of perplexed eyes looked at her askance.

"Alright, that's enough girls! Sit down and I'll explain." *Mausi*, clearly fed up with the questions, decided to come clean.

"*Biji* isn't just some stray woman we've picked up off the streets. She comes from a very respectable family. Her father and Papa's father were good friends. In fact, her son and Papa went to the same school, were in the same class even."

"*Biji*'s husband died while she was quite young, and she brought up her son, single handedly on her husband's pension and from selling off a lot of her jewellery and lands. She even sent Manav to America to study. When he came back to India, he landed a really good job, got married and things seemed to be going well for them. *Biji* thought all her days of struggle were behind her."

Tara shifted uncomfortably on the sofa. This story was a bit too long winded for her. Ruchi leaned forward, fascinated.

"Manav always hankered to return to America. He thought there was no future for him and his girls here. His wife agreed with him. *Biji* was the only one who insisted on living in India. This led to many rows between them. In the end, Manav convinced her and they decided to emigrate to the US."

"What happened then?"

"*Biji* sold the house, the last of her jewellery and lands to fund the move. They left for the airport with all their worldly possessions. They sat her down on a seat and told her they would check in and come back to get her. They never did."

2007

RUCHI rang Tara the same evening.

"What happened?"

"She had a fall. Hit her head on the edge of the wash basin and that was it."

"Oh Tara, I'm so sorry! How awful... When had you seen her last?"

"The last time I was in Delhi, which was around six months ago. Can you imagine, she still carried that old photo around on her?"

"Did she say anything?"

"No, Ruchi. She never spoke, remember? I think the shock of what that horrible son of hers did was too much for her."

"I wish ... I wish..."

"I know, honey. I wish we could have done more too. But strangely, I think we may have. She saw us as her substitute grand-daughters and I think our times with her did give her some kind of happiness, however little it may have been."

"How did *Mausi* and *Mausa* take it?"

"They were upset of course, but it was Ramu who took it real hard. He's been locked up in his room all day, refusing to eat. He was really fond of her."

"You okay?"

"Sad, lonely, a bit fed up with the job. You?"

"Yeah, same. Mummy's not been too well, and she keeps talking about moving to Dehradun."

"Hmmm. And your dad?"

"On his third marriage. Don't even ask. So, are you going for the cremation?"

"Yes, I am. She was family, after all."

15

___

FALLEN

Who could have predicted this? Except the *Devas*[1]. The Gods who must be chortling into their *Somras*[2].

I am indestructible. My knowledge surpasses all, my physical prowess is second to none. I have sipped on the nectar of immortality. I have been a fair and just ruler. My people want for nothing. They suffer no deprivation. Yet, with the foresight I have been blessed with, I know that all this will mean nothing one day. One day, I will be made a mockery of. Grotesque effigies of me will be burnt publicly to celebrate the defeat of evil. I will come to represent all that is wicked, greedy, arrogant and worthy of destruction.

They will forget that I am the *Maha Brahman*[3]- called thus by their own Lord.

I wait in solitude for Death to arrive. It frightens me not a jot. For I have chosen this fate for myself. In abducting the beauteous queen, I have provided enough incentive for the Lord to bring his army here to my land, and for me to be felled by his hand. It is the only way for me to gain *Moksha* - an emancipation from this cycle of death and rebirth.

The queen sits in her own solitude in the garden. I captured her as a means to an end. Yet, I find, that it is I who is enraptured of her.

She, who waits so patiently for her husband to rescue her. She, who waits for my defeat. Can she even guess at the trials that lie ahead of her? That she will have to walk through fire to prove her chastity. That she will be turned out, pregnant and helpless, on the accusation of a washerman. I treat her with respect and with dignity. She scoffs at my love, but someday she will recall that it is not I, but her own revered Lord that cast doubt on her virtue.

As dusk gives way to an inky night, I look up at the stars, and find that I am ready to leave this mortal coil. Whatever my legacy may come to mean, I will never be forgotten. For hundreds of years they will celebrate the return of the rightful King to his Kingdom by lighting *diyas*[4] and distributing sweetmeats. But not before they mark my annihilation.

For I am Ravana, and the story of Rama and Sita and *The Ramayana*[5] will not exist without me.

LIKE A BOSS

"*Aaj kal tere mere pyar ke charchey har zubaan par...*"[1] Raju's voice goes up an octave as the girl passes him by, the evergreen Hindi song declaring their mutual love to the world. His eyes roam over her person, ignoring the withering look she throws him as she readjusts her *dupatta*[2] over her chest. She quickens her pace trying to get away from his lecherous examination of her. He's already moved on to the next woman on the street. Oof! This one is an auntie-*ji* variety. He can't be bothered with her.

Nine o'clock in the morning is a busy time with people hurrying to get to work or to their businesses. Raju has parked himself on a low wall, his satchel thrown beside him. He is meant to be in college instead he loiters here. As long as he gets the necessary amount of attendance, what does it matter? It is so much more fun, sitting here and teasing the young women as they walk past.

He is waiting for her, the special one. Her father is a policeman and he knows he could get into so much trouble if she ever reported him. But as she hasn't so far, it leads him to believe she likes him back. Girls are such teases anyway. They never say what's on their minds. They draw you in, then push you away. They play silly games and expect you to understand them.

"Haramzaadi, khaana bhi theek se nahin bana sakti?! Kutti kahin ki! Idhar aa....aaj toh teri taang todh ke chodhunga....[3]!" Baba hitting Amma. Her muffled apologies. His wrath. Then their lovemaking. Soft moans and grunts that he tries to shut out but can't. His brother lying in bed with him, trembling in fear, praying that their father is worn out and doesn't turn upon them later. Their mother, the morning after, covered in bruises, seeing her husband off lovingly, refusing to meet her sons' eyes.

She walks past him, her head held high, her body stiffened in anticipation of his verbal assault. First, he whistles, then licks his lips lasciviously. Finally, he launches into another song: *"Aaja aaja mein hoon pyar tera..."* [4]

She ignores him completely, like he doesn't exist, like he's a bit of cowpat by the side of the street. Bitch!

He clambers off the wall and follows her.

"Eh madam? Madam?"

She looks at him. *"Kya[5]?"*

"Dogi[6]?"

Her eyes widen as comprehension dawns on her. He's asking if she'll fuck him. One word is all it takes. Disgusted, she walks away. He grins, his thrill complete.

HIS FRIENDS ARE WAITING for him outside the college. None of them are the studious types. This isn't a college the studious types go to anyway.

"Aey Raju, where were you *bhai[7]*? We've been waiting for ages..." Nitin is stubbing his cigarette out on the tree.

"Just checking the girls out near Mata Devi college. Man, I could tear their *salwars* off and take them on the street."

"Shut up you horny bastard! Who is going to fuck you, you five foot nothing?" Salim loves to put him down.

Raju glares at him. "You can talk, *chutiye[8]*. You've been fucking that cousin of yours for how many years now? Keeping it in the family, hey?"

"Enough, enough!" Kapil is the peace keeper in their group. Older by a few years, no one knows whether he actually even belongs to the college or just comes to hang around. Since he supplies them with alcohol, cigarettes and dirty magazines, no one cares to question him further.

"What happened to the drugs you were going to bring us, Kapil?" Nitin asks, lighting up another cigarette. His teeth are brown from chain smoking and he is reed thin.

"*Arey sallon*[9], you can't afford to piss in a pot and you're asking for drugs? Be content with the stuff I do bring you. The rest is for the rich kids on the North campus."

It's shitty being poor. They are not *poor* poor but they are lower middle class. In a city as affluent as Delhi that means no cars, no drugs, no money and no girlfriends. Even their college is an all-male prison where only the homos get laid.

"Shukla is giving a lecture today. Want to go in?" Salim occasionally displays a desire to learn.

"What for? Not like we're going to sit for the IAS.[10] You're going to inherit your father's garage. A lecture on ethics isn't going to make you a better mechanic." Nitin is spot on, as usual.

"*Aey*, let's go to the new mall that's opened. Bet there'll be some pretty girls there!" Raju says.

"Yeah, pretty, rich girls who won't give *you* a second glance! Raju, when are you going to learn?"

NEVERTHELESS, they traipse over to the new mall. They walk past the shop fronts that display wares with prices that are more than the rents their parents pay. They peek into the Men's department, eyeing the expensive jackets and cufflinks while the security guard follows them around, glowering every time they touch something. Nitin puts on a pair of Ray-Ban sunglasses, admiring his reflection in the mirror. He spots something stuck in his teeth and uses the long nail of his pinky finger to pull it out.

"If I had money, I would look like a Boss. Better than that Ranvir Seth actor. I tell you, money is everything."

They all nod in unison.

They wander over to the Perfume department and start spraying themselves with the testers.

A girl in an ill-fitting black jacket comes over to them.

"Sir, these are ladies perfumes."

"So?" Kapil postures, cringing inwardly. He should have known better.

They meander out, much to the relief of the staff. They head to McDonalds and sit down.

"Eh, one of us will have to get something or they'll throw us out!"

Nitin takes out his newly acquired Ray-Bans, puts them on and saunters towards the counter to order a milkshake.

"He's fucking got guts! If they'd caught him shoplifting, we'd all be in jail right now..." Salim states this with a grudging admiration.

They pass the milkshake around. It's like liquefied ice cream.

"How these rich people don't get fat, I don't know. If this is the kind of stuff they eat and drink all the time."

"*Arey*,[11] all Americans are fat. That's where this shit comes from."

"No, they're not. Haven't you seen them on TV? Skinny women with huge boobs."

"Those are plastic."

"What? The boobs?"

"Yeah man, they fill them with silicone or something. Keeps them upright."

"Hey, hey, look at this one just coming in..."

They all turn to stare at the girl who has just walked in. Her black jeans are skin tight, and the T shirt is stretched across her chest.

"Why is she wearing a T shirt saying 'Bitch'"?

"You *gadhé*[12]! It says 'Fitch'. It's some American designer."

They keep examining her, each of them mentally undressing her. She flicks her hair back as she waits for her order. Her lips are painted a vixen red and her long nails have burgundy nail varnish on them. She taps away on her gold phone barely looking up as the boy behind the counter asks her a question.

She sits down two tables across from them. The counter boy places her tray in front of her, pocketing the Rs,50 she tips him.

"So, she gets special service?" Nitin remarks sourly.

Raju doesn't respond. He's getting hard just looking at her. This is the kind of girl he wants to lose his virginity to. Sweet smelling, curvy, expensive.

Salim looks at him, looking at her. "Go try your luck, *bhosdee kay*[13]. Just staring won't get you anywhere."

They egg him on, so he gets up and approaches her. She looks up from her phone as he sits across from her.

"You are very beautiful…" he stutters.

"What do you want?" She glares at him.

"Number. Phone number."

She looks at him up and down, then starts laughing. Suddenly, not knowing how or why, he reaches across the table and squeezes her boob. She screams and then everything is a blur.

They are outside, being beaten by security guards and a large, muscular guy who seems to be her boyfriend.

"*Jaanu*[14]… *Jaanu*…" She keeps crying, trying to pull him off.

He feels the kicks, the slaps, the punches all over his body and cowers. A trickle between his legs and he knows he has wet himself again.

He is fifteen and being beaten by Baba for some infraction. He loses control of his bladder and suddenly there is a pool of piss under their feet. Baba hits him harder calling him a 'napunsak[15]*'. Then he knees him in the groin with a savage satisfaction. As Raju falls to the floor, he sees his mother mop up his urine.*

SALIM IS HOLDING an ice pack to his head while Kapil dabs at his wounds with Dettol. Nitin is staring out of the window, the cigarette smouldering between his fingers. Raju sits on the bed, a towel wrapped around his waist while his jeans and underwear dry on the washing line on the terrace.

This is the first time they've been to Kapil's flat. He lives alone, but they are surprised to find how neat and clean it is. He even has a vase with fresh flowers in it.

"I think today is a whiskey kind of day." Kapil declares as he fetches a bottle of McDowell's and four steel tumblers. "We have to get very, very drunk."

Nothing alleviates the pain and humiliation of a thrashing like whiskey. They are slurring their words now, trying to pull Raju's towel off, rolling around on the floor, laughing for no good reason.

Salim's phone rings at some point and he shushes them, putting his finger to his lips and looking fierce. He mutters into the phone while they drunkenly try to pull him to the floor.

"*Haan Abba*[16]. Yes, yes." His head is nodding alongside as though reinforcing the affirmatives rolling off his tongue.

"I have to go. *Abba*[17] is going for a meeting and there is no cover at the garage."

They protest, they try to hold on to him and then drunkenly insist that they will all go together. Raju hops around on one leg trying to put his jeans on. They seem to have shrunk.

"Idiot!" Nitin has tears running down his face, he is laughing so hard. "You're putting them on backwards..."

THE FRESH AIR sobers them up enough to ride the DTC bus to Salim's garage in a fair show of temperance. Still, people seem to give them a wide berth. Raju likes it. He feels powerful suddenly, as though he owns this bus. Like a Boss. Nitin gives him a drunken wink and all at once he is overcome with affection for his friends. True mates. They will live and die together. Who needs fucking women?

They loll around the cars admiring the foreign ones.

"Have you ever driven a BMW, Salim?"

"No, but I drove a Mercedes once. Put a big dent in it. *Abba* nearly killed me!"

"Why is there a bus parked outside?"

"Oh, that's Ishfaq *bhai'*[18]s bus. He has several private ones. He rents them out to wedding parties. This one, I think, is a school bus. *Abba's* just fixed the radiator on it."

"Hey!" Nitin exclaims. "Let's drive it."

"What? No way, man. *Abba* will have my hide."

"Come on! We'll have it back by 9pm. It's only seven o' clock right now."

Kapil pulls out another bottle of whiskey. "Come on Salim, it'll be fun. Let's see what these private school kids feel like, being ferried on a bus. Only, we'll be driving it." He motions turning a large steering wheel, grinning maniacally.

They take turns at the wheel. All of them except Raju, who cannot drive. So, he pretends to be the conductor, running up and down the aisle, selling tickets to phantom passengers.

They drive to the outskirts of the city, weaving drunkenly in between rush hour traffic. Raju sticks his head out of an open window and yells "I'm a BOSS! Yeah...a BOSS!!" Nitin pulls him back in before he is decapitated by an electricity pole.

They pass the whiskey around, drinking it straight from the bottle. No tumblers between them and the good stuff. There is an iron rod laying on the last row of the bus and Salim picks it up like it is a sword and he is Akbar, the all-powerful emperor of India. He marches with the sword held aloft, till he runs it through his enemy who just happens to be Nitin, who mock collapses on Raju while Kapil takes a sharp turn and they all fall upon each other, laughing, breathless.

It's dark outside and they are back in the city. The traffic has thinned a bit and the street lights seem to have a warm halo around them. Kapil reduces his speed sensing their mood. They are all reluctant to end their adventure. It's coming up to nine o'clock. Raju wonders if anyone is missing him at home.

They are passing by the big cinema complex when Nitin spots them. A couple in their early twenties. Boyfriend and girlfriend. Or husband and wife? The young man is trying to flag down transport.

"Slow down," he whispers to Kapil. He looks over at Raju. "Want to have some more fun?"

They stop the bus near the couple. Salim and Nitin are pretending to be passengers. Raju leans out of the bus *"Kahaan jaana hai*[19]*?"*

"Vikaspuri." The young man answers while the young woman looks at the bus suspiciously. She is nodding her head, trying to say something to him.

"Aa jao didi. Pahuncha dengé.[20]*"*

MAYBE IT's the fact that he calls her sister, maybe it's the fact that he looks a lot younger than his nineteen years, maybe it's the fact that they are desperate, but they get in.

She climbs in first followed by the man. At once, he can tell, she knows something is wrong. She has smelled the alcohol or seen the drawn curtains on the windows of the cavernous bus. She spins around as Salim hits the man on the head with the iron rod. Her face turns pale as she realises what is about to happen. She launches herself at Raju, clawing at his face, screaming for help. She puts up one hell of a fight. She bites, she scratches, she howls, she struggles with all her might, but Kapil is once again on the outskirts of the city and no one can hear her. The boyfriend/husband is knocked out cold. They take it in turns to rape her. All except Kapil who is still driving. Then Salim takes the wheel and Kapil comes over.

Strangely excited, Raju watches Kapil unzip himself. He rubs his penis to harden it, but nothing happens. The woman is weaving in and out of consciousness. Kapil looks up, embarrassed. "It's the whiskey..." Raju pushes him aside and climbs on top of her again. He inserts himself in her, moaning with pleasure. Nitin is holding her down, his trousers still unbuttoned in readiness for his turn. She regains consciousness and starts struggling once more, screaming, crying, begging...

"Shut her up!" Salim shouts from the wheel.

Nitin slaps her hard then puts his hand on her mouth saying, "Shut up, you whore!" He looks up at Kapil and smirks. "Not going to fuck her? Want to fuck him instead?" He jerks his head towards the unconscious man.

Kapil lurches angrily towards Nitin and grabs the iron rod from behind him. He pushes Raju off the woman and viciously shoves the rod inside her.

"There are ways and *ways* to fuck!" Her body jerks involuntarily and she screams in agony, but Kapil keeps pushing, staring Nitin in the eye, as though engaged in some private duel.

They reach the edge of a farmland and Salim comes to a halt.

"Get them out. We have to clean the bus before returning it to the garage."

They drag the couple's unconscious bodies from the bus and throw them both outside, then get back in. Nitin and Kapil retire to two different corners of the bus. Salim pulls away cautiously. Dawn is breaking, and the orange rays of the early morning sun fall upon the ears of corn, as though setting them on fire.

The bus drives away and Raju looks back to see the two bodies lying by the side of the road like broken puppets. He turns around, closes his eyes, lays his head back on the seat and falls asleep instantly.

Sign up today to hear of Poornima's new releases and promotions!

AFTERWORD

Word-of-mouth is crucial for any author to succeed and if you found this book interesting *please* do leave a review on your preferred site. Even if it's just a star rating or a sentence or two, it would make all the difference and would be very much appreciated!!

If you enjoyed this book, you can sign up to hear more about my new releases and any special offers!

Do visit www.poornimamanco.com to keep abreast of all my news.

ALSO BY POORNIMA MANCO

Parvathy's Well & other stories

Holi Moly! & other stories

The Intimacy of Loss

Twelve - stories from around the world

Parvathy's Well & Other Stories: The India Collection

A Quiet Dissonance

GLOSSARY OF TERMS

1. Damage

1. Blouse
2. Uncle, normally mother's brother
3. Uncle, normally mother's brother
4. Fried bread stuffed with egg

2. Samsara

1. Boss
2. Police Station
3. Big boss
4. Boss
5. Who is it?
6. All of them are pussies!
7. A term indicating respect
8. Kohl
9. Film
10. Tea
11. Mother
12. Lentil curry from South India
13. Steamed savoury rice cake
14. Lentil curry from South India
15. Poetry
16. A savoury pancake
17. Nepalese curved knife

4. Ma Vie Sans Couleur

1. Gardener

5. Secrets And Lies

1. Elder sister
2. The ingredients required for ritual offerings
3. Prayers

4. The long end of the sari, worn over the shoulder
5. Grandfather
6. Indian sweet made of ghee, sugar, gram flour and cardamom
7. Father

6. The Consequence Of Contradiction

1. The long end of the sari, worn over the shoulder
2. Beauty rituals
3. Uncle, mother's brother
4. Uncle's wife
5. Lentil curry and Indian flatbread
6. Spices
7. Seasoning
8. Indian flat bread
9. Child, generic usage

7. Love Jihad

1. Mother
2. Father
3. Tea
4. A light bedstead
5. A religious slogan
6. Heavenly Nectar
7. Brother (respectful)
8. Muslims
9. Followers
10. Elder sister
11. Indian street games
12. Indian street games
13. Child, generic usage
14. Vagina/pussy used as a swear word
15. Bitch
16. Child, generic usage
17. Wedding
18. Elder sister
19. Shopkeeper
20. The long end of the sari, worn over the shoulder
21. A dark horse
22. Prayers
23. Pal (slang)
24. Mother's sister

25. Urdu couplet by poet Amn Lakhnavi loosely translated as: Life is a question which has only Death as the answer; Death too, is a question, but it has no answer.

9. Swami Claus

1. Elder sister
2. Vow of silence
3. Indian milk sweet

10. Ugly

1. A musical instrument played at weddings
2. Decorated and embellished shoes
3. Plate
4. A respectful yes
5. A casual expression equivalent to 'Hey'
6. An Indian prayer chant called the Gayatri Mantra
7. Tea
8. An Indian prayer chant, normally recited at cremations

11. Palindrome

1. Mother
2. Daughter
3. Soldier
4. Betel quid chewed as a digestive
5. A long, loose top
6. Tiffin carriers
7. Salt

12. Dear Anil

1. A cloth bag
2. Indian loose shirt top and trousers
3. Hair worn in a loose bun
4. Sister-like, a term used to denote plainness

14. The Strings That Bind Us

1. Indian comic books popular in the 70's/80's
2. Indian comic books popular in the 70's/80's
3. Elder sister, generic usage
4. Brother
5. Room on the flat roof of an Indian home
6. Cheap cigarettes
7. Okra
8. Mother's sister
9. Mother's sister's husband
10. Room on the flat roof of an Indian home
11. Temple
12. A little lamp
13. A sweet of some kind, considered a blessing from God
14. A small seat
15. Now
16. Glass
17. Prayer plate
18. Father's younger brother, used in a general way here to denote respect for an elderly male servant
19. Roosters
20. An Indian sweet
21. Grandmother, generic usage
22. Grandmother - Mother's mother
23. Indian sweet
24. Goddess Saraswati, the goddess of education

15. Fallen

1. Gods
2. Heavenly Nectar
3. The most learned of all Brahmins
4. Little lamps
5. an ancient Indian epic poem which narrates the struggle of the divine prince Rama to rescue his wife Sita from the demon king Ravana.

16. Like A Boss

1. Popular Hindi song
2. Scarf
3. You bitch, you can't even cook properly? Come here, I'll break your leg today...
4. Old Hindi film song

5. What?
6. Will you give out?
7. Brother
8. Cunt (swear word)
9. You losers
10. Indian Administrative Services
11. Hey
12. Ass
13. Son of a whore
14. Darling
15. Impotent man
16. Yes Father
17. Father
18. Brother
19. Where do you want to go?
20. Get in sister. We'll take you to your destination.

Acknowledgments

1. A very big thank you to you!

ACKNOWLEDGMENTS

Writing is a solitary occupation. Yet, bringing a book to the reader is a collaborative effort. In rejecting the traditional route of agent, publisher and marketing junkets, I have had to assemble my own little team and it is to them that I owe my maximum thanks.

My beta readers who I chose because both are avid readers, hail from the same sort of background as I do and are very close friends. I knew, without a doubt, that they wouldn't hesitate to call me on any of my BS and would happily point out the things they disliked about the stories. Well, I got that in spades!

Vani Viswanathan, my first beta reader did not mince words when it came to certain stories. Not all the tales were to her liking but she ploughed through them regardless, pointing out errors and discrepancies along the way. She helped me view the stories from another perspective, the perspective of a reader who is not immediately in love with all that I write. Criticism can hurt but criticism is essential for a writer to grow and develop. Through Vani's eyes I saw the old adage come true - 'one man's meat is another man's poison'. Thank you Vani for not holding back. Thank you for still keeping the faith through all our spats and misunderstandings. I do hope you enjoy the final version of the book.

Vibha Sharma, my other beta reader, was gentler in her criticism. She is, what I would call, my ideal reader, purely because she completely 'gets' my stories. She understands the darkness within them just as she understands what I am trying to achieve in telling these stories. However, she brought a much needed clarity to the order of the tales. In making me rejig the sequence, she showed me how important it is to draw the reader in slowly to the heart of darkness, not plunge them straight in, flailing and gasping for breath. Her help was invaluable in deciding where the mellower, more placid and meandering tales should be positioned to allow the short, sharp and horrid stories to have maximum impact. Thank you Vibha, I still owe you that drink!

My proofreaders come next: Pearl Csuk and Eileen Nahum - how can I possibly thank you for taking time out of your hectic lives to pore over my manuscript? The errors you found and corrected, the spelling mistakes, the grammar and the 'Indianisms' that didn't quite cut it, were diligently set down for me. As for my final proofreader, the incomparable Jyoti Bhargava, who patiently added and subtracted my random commas and pointed out my strange fondness for ellipses, *aapka bahut bahut dhanyawaad*[1]! I was too close to the material to see any of it and if it weren't for all your help, the manuscript would still have been a mewling kitten as opposed to a prowling cat.

Also, a big thank you to my husband and daughters. When the job I do takes me away for days at a time, it is all the more difficult to deal with a wife/mother who is physically present but completely unavailable while she is tap tapping away on her laptop. Thank you Mike for the number of times you stepped in to make dinner because I had completely lost track of time. Thank you for putting up with my mood swings and snapping-your-head-off moments when I was struggling with a character trajectory. You may not be much of a reader (although, of course, you will be forced at knife point to read this book) but you have always been my supporter and champion.

My girls - Mahika and Prianka - thank you for having the patience to sit and read some of mummy's stories even though you'd much rather have been listening to and dancing along with K-pop. Dark and depressing is not really your thing but you read them anyway and cheered me on. Mahika, you my darling, are developing into quite the literary critic. The number of times you helped me wittingly and unwittingly are too numerous to recount. A big kiss for Prianka who helped me with my formatting and all computer related glitches.

Finally, the biggest thanks goes out to the people who buy and read this book. If it weren't for you readers, all these stories would mean nothing.

ABOUT THE AUTHOR

A bookworm since childhood, her imagination was channelled into writing by her mother. She won several competitions at School and University for her writing but never pursued it seriously. After several years of a writing hiatus, akin to being in writing Siberia, a competition in a newspaper reignited her love. The outcome was Parvathy's Well.

That story remains special as it once again set her on the path to writing, and reacquainting herself with her dormant creative self.

She lives and works in the United Kingdom, is married and has two teenage daughters.

You can follow her thoughts and musings at:
www.poornimamanco.com

9 781916 269972